Brian Case

is a writer, journalist, and Senior Editor of *Time Out* Magazine. *The Users* is his first novel and was initially published in 1968. He lives in Kent with his wife Sonia and their two daughters.

The Users

A NOVEL BY

BRIAN CASE

THE DO-NOT PRESS

Published in Great Britain in 1996 by
The Do-Not Press
PO Box 4215
London SE23 2QD

Copyright © 1968/renewed 1996 by Brian Case
All rights reserved

Originally published by Peter Davies, London

ISBN 1 899344 05 5

British Library Cataloguing in Publication Data. A catalogue record for
this book is available from the British Library.

Printed and bound in Great Britain by The Guernsey Press Co Ltd,
Guernsey, Channel Islands

To Sonia,
Daisy and Molly.

Part One

1

It was the first time they had used a tape-recorder in the morgue. Mr Reed was very excited. He polished all the instruments, pulled out the drawers of the refrigerator and combed everybody's hair. His eyes kept wandering over to the tape-recorder.

The pathologist would arrive at 4pm to conduct his examination, this time recording his method and his findings, for the instruction of the medical students in the hospital. Mr Reed saw that he had twenty minutes in which to prepare for the session. The body lay naked and yellow under the bright, tented lights. A label tied to the left big toe read: *Sydney Jenkins*.

Mr Reed circled the porcelain table, scalpel poised like one mean spic bopper searching for an opening. Mr Reed made his own. He inserted the scalpel at the throat and drew a line down to the navel, then from there two lines to the groin to form an ultra-committed CND badge. With gloved fingers he pulled the wound open to expose the rib-cage. Experience told him that the saw would be unnecessary; the body was old and the bones would be fairly brittle. He selected a small knife from the range of instruments and applied it to the ribs, cutting out and removing a square of rib-cage like a trapdoor to reveal the lungs. Now Mr Reed again took up the scalpel and turned his attention to the head. He opened the mouth, pinched the tongue delicately between thumb and forefinger and severed the membrane securing it. He drew the tongue and trachea out through the new throat opening and onto the chest. And that was that. Mr Reed had few friends.

He stripped off the rubber gloves and leaned against the table. Normally he would have trepanned the corpse but the report had stated that the cause of death was drowning. Mr Reed was inclined to disagree. No signs of mucus foam around the nose and mouth; the hands, stiff of course, but not technically clutched. Anyway, if the doctor wanted to examine the cranium he would say so.

He padded on crêpe soles to the tape-recorder and lifted the lid. He looked inside; everything seemed in order to him though of course his forté lay elsewhere. Gingerly, his finger winkled the microphone out of its niche and uncoiled the lead; his fingertips seemed to respond to an habitual pattern — only the names were changed. He followed the instructions printed on the lid, and got the instrument ready for use. The doctor was due to arrive in a few minutes.

Crossing to the cupboard he removed two pairs of white wellingtons, two rubber aprons, two back-to-front overalls and a box of surgical gloves, dusted with talcum and rolled inside out.

'Funny thing,' he mused, unpacking the gloves, 'there's rolled-on rubbers at your beginning and rolled-on rubbers at your end. Ironic !' Thus Mr Reed bethought himself of man's estate, gliding effortlessly over schism and logic, as the outer door closed with a padded and pneumatic wheeze.

'Afternoon Mr Reed,' the doctor called breezily, divesting himself of hat and coat in the very act of entry.

'Good afternoon doctor,' said Mr Reed.

The doctor scooped up the report and read it, his sandy eyebrows twitching like riders over his eyes.

'Uh-huh,' he said at intervals, and 'Mmm', while Mr Reed ensnared his blind outstretched arms in an overall. The row of clothing diminished in direct proportion to his increasingly vestal appearance.

'Yep,' said the doctor, throwing the report onto the table. 'Conjecture, Mr Reed. All bloody conjecture. Presumed cause of death — estimated length of immersion — the rescuers alleged. Where would they be without us, Mr Reed? Buggered, Mr Reed.'

Mr Reed, a coat-hanger dependent from his fingers, in the act of hanging a jacket, judicially nodded.

'Did the machine come — the tape-recorder? Ah yes. Turn the thing on — and we'd better have the microphone thing — er' he glanced for the first time at the body on the table — 'oh there you are — yes, put it between his knees.'

Mr Reed complied gravely, his heart singing within him, as he cleared his throat of extraneous mucus and incanted from one to ten. He played the result back; it was perfect. He seized the microphone again and began — 'Ten, nine, eight…'

'No, no, Mr Reed, I think we can assume that it's working satisfactorily from those initial soundings.' The doctor plunged his hands into the open body and interspersed fleshly squeakings with commentary in a You-are-there sort of technique.

'We know that the body is seventy years of age, male and reasonably healthy — er — up till the er — yes. *Presumed* cause of death — drowning. Condition of body *suggests* a duration of between one and two hours in the water. No signs of significant bruising or breaking etcetera. The lungs are free of water as indeed they would be if he had drowned. Asphyxia, of course. We'd better have a look at the cranium.'

'Shall I commence to 'trepan, doctor?' Mr Reed spoke in a strange nasal voice.

The doctor stared at his assistant. 'I didn't notice that his head was transparent, Mr Reed.'

The doctor switched off the tape-recorder and watched Mr Reed at work on the head; his face was arranged in a careful blank, his hands worked swiftly and surely. The doctor was sorry for his sarcasm; perhaps it was the presence of the noiseless third party; he had never transgressed the code of professional ethics before. 'You have educated fingers, Mr Reed,' he said.

Mr Reed looked up, his face flushed and smiling. 'We can learn something from even the most ordinary lump of flesh, eh Doctor?' he said. 'It's all useful.'

'Do you want to see him sir?' asked Mr Reed when John had signed for the carrier bag. He indicated the sheet-covered trolley in the chapel.

Most of the time the chapel was used for tea breaks by Mr Reed and the technicians from the path' lab. The removal of ashtrays and the biscuit-buying roster from the wall made a big difference, no two ways about it, and setting up the plain wooden cross on the table was a visible staking out, no disrespect, of The

Lord's claim. Nevertheless, he worried. It should be harder than that. And — he could see two ways about it.

John said, 'No thank you. Can I leave it for a while?'

Mr Reed discreetly withdrew and sat against the far wall to leave him to his grief. Oh yes — it was all right for the others to guzzle their tea in here and do their pools. They never saw the room when it was a chapel, but he did. He did, and it put him off his biscuits. Mr Reed had worried about the problem for ten years and had turned to his Bible for advice, combing in vain for an Eastern parallel. He had likened the path. lab. technicians to the moneylenders in the temple before the unfairness of this occurred to him. It just wasn't that simple. Bursting in the door and flailing about with plaited drainage tubes would solve nothing, besides being presumptuous. Simply it came to this: he did not know when the room stopped being a temple, chapel, and started being a place for tea breaks. How significant was the movement of furniture? He looked at his watch and saw that it would be tea break in twenty minutes. More lugging about.

'Take your time sir,' he said, a foxy jostle. 'I know how it is to lose somebody. You just let me know when you're ready to view.'

'Thank you,' said John and continued to just stand.

Hospital sounds, the breezy confident sounds of people halfway through the working day, colleagues in corridors, containers clanking, faintly reverberated against the double doors. John stood in the centre of the room facing the trolley, the cross on the table, the curtained window, and in that poor grey light there seemed to be no appreciable distance between them.

Mr Reed, sitting respectfully, small banjo-shaped shoes pressed together, knees touching, absented himself in his problem. A year ago at the union meeting he had suggested, all heads turning towards him, that they have the room sprinkled by a bishop. General laughter; ignorant laughter; that would put the mockers on the tea breaks. Render unto Caesar, he had warned them and they had laughed loudly and called him Creeping Jesus among themselves. He frowned, remembering it.

The Egyptians removed the brains through the nose. Mr Reed admired the Egyptians for their diligence, patience and skill and he thought of them now to avoid thinking of his own bumbling ineptitude in settling the status of the room. It was easy for the Egyptians though. They had jam on it. No-one was likely to confuse a pyramid with a tea room. Sprinkle three walls and then sit back for the next three thousand years: in his mind's eye he watched them file silently past silent bandaged upright corpses and out into the hot bustling day, straining black backs and *Clunk* — the final stone. All sealed off. Nice. Proper. Not like this, he thought bitterly. Chopping and changing, never knowing where you were. No — wait a mo'. You knew where you were but you didn't know what it was where you were... A very nice point. Bang it in the diary at tea break.

He looked up at the mourner and saw that his eyes were dry and his face, profile, was completely still. Mr Reed had seen that before. They were the ones to watch, the awkward ones. All quiet at first, hypnotised as it were, then all of a sudden — Boom! throw themselves on the body, screaming and laughing, spitty kisses all over, breaking the stitches, hell of a job. He shifted uneasily on his chair.

John was thinking about curtains, the curtains at the window. They were a completely unremarkable floral print, the stereotype of a million drawing-rooms, yet, strangely, they fascinated him. He wondered why. Was it perhaps that the windows they partly screened were frosted, needing none, redundant as water in a vase of plastic flowers? No, he didn't think it was that. It came to him then that it was their very unremarkableness that held him fixed. The curtains created a context that jarred hideously with the thing on the trolley and it seemed to him that it was here, in this room, as quiet and curtained against calamity as the drawing-room of his home, that his father had died. This was the very room of empty Sundays, of switch click and clock tick, where suddenly a monstrous hysteria had exploded, hatchet blade rising falling flinging black beads up the wallpaper, covering even the *Radio Times* with gore. The flashbulbs of police photographers, the note-takers, the doctors, the fingerprint men, chalk lines on the floor like an amulet against evil, all raced through his mind before he found what he was groping for: that no-one need ever seek a motive in such a room.

All of which was, he reflected, a fairly typical excursion for his imagination, through landscape habitually hothouse and ornamental.

Mr Reed decided to take the initiative so he stood up and said: 'Are you ready to view, sir?'

'All right,' said John and at once felt the inadequacy of the words. 'I am prepared,' he amended.

The attendant's shoes squeaked across the lino, wincing as it were with a sense of occasion. John fixed his eyes on the white contours of the sheet, a little nervous because he had never seen a dead body. The attendant swept the sheet aside in a perfect veronica so that the body was uncovered to the waist. John gasped, not because the face was frightening — it was, as in life, uncommunicative — but because he had expected to see it a good twelve inches higher. He had taken the lump of the pillow for the head under the sheet and now he had to re-adjust. In that moment the face had swum into the periphery of his tensed, directed gaze, ghostlike and in stealth.

'He looks just the same,' he said in an over-loud voice but he knew that he didn't. His father looked fuller-faced, healthier, generally better; in fact, he thought, preferable.

'Oh yes, they do. This is only the earth suit,' replied Mr Reed, but experiencing nonetheless pride in his work. The toothless mouth padded out with cotton wool, the cochineal injection in the cheeks for rosiness, the small, neat, uniform stitches concealed by the hair; all the little things that came only with twenty years of experience. He smiled sadly at the corpse and felt a warm sympathy for the young man who had turned out to be, after all, just a quiet type paying his respects as a son.

'He wasn't drowned, sir. He fell and hit his head. It was mercifully quick. The police said he'd climbed under the jetty to cut his line free and then slipped and fallen.'

John stared at the body. 'The hair,' he said suddenly. 'You've got his hair all wrong. He never had a parting there.' With splayed fingers he reached out to take the hair back from the brow, but he could not bring himself to touch his father. He let his hand fall limply back to his side. After all, he told himself, his father had been a scruffy old bastard when he was alive, so let him go on with it.

'If I'd had a photo to go on...' Mr Reed murmured, watching him, expecting something now. John crackled the carrier bag, changing his grip, embarrassed.

'I'm sorry. I'm not criticising...' he cleared his throat.

Mr Reed covered the body again and crossing, steered him by the elbow to the door, concealing the gentle pressure with assurances and platitudes. Life, he thought, as the doors closed behind the mourner, was so full of uncertainties. You never can tell. He opened his diary and licked the pencil stub, but before he could write, a horrible thought struck him. If he had the room done, consecrated, and they carried on borrowing it for a tea room, would the digestives become The Body and the tea...? He couldn't bear to think about it. It was so horrible that he stood up and went into the post-mortem room.

As the glass doors closed behind him John Jenkins took a deep breath, filling his lungs like people did in films to show they value life anew. Or have big tits, he thought. It was raining hard. He turned up the collar of his combat jacket, two pound ten US surplus, supply your own combat, and ran through the hospital parking lot into the street. Bashing through the puddles it occurred to him that he ought to be photographed now, straight away while the ravages of grief were still hot on his features. Bang it in the old album with date and circumstance. He ran down the darkening street until he could see the dark bulk of the railway station and the unfortunate double steeple, a rudeness unto the Man, of St Christopher's; the automatic photo-booth was opposite the vestry, very handy for post-service, high-key, nimbus extra snapstrips.

Office workers poured out of offices into the street, wild-eyed and hell-bent for home, all elbows and umbrellas but a very regular army. Everybody peeled off from the pacamass along dotted lines of departure, jostling no-one as they bought papers and boarded buses. John moved in mambo and foxtrot through them, demurely dipping his headlights for approaching dollies. He was in the habit of staring lustfully up to ten yards and then turning chicken, but he did pick up on the perfumed slip-stream as they passed, thinking of the little parachute of essence and its tale of dusted nooks and peppered crannies. Today, the rain made it extra nice: damp nooks, damp crannies: himself perhaps Terry Towelling, the fleecy frotteur.

He cursed the lights that kept him jigging at the kerb in the rain. Some of the office workers took a chance and ran to the island. John could see they were mad. Only a fool would trust a replica. Replicas of people were drawn on all three sides of the windscreen and windows as on children's toys but they didn't fool him. John played it dose to the chest, waiting until he had solid bumpers of pedestrians, ranks of statistics (cars only killed statistics) on every side of him before conveying his quick kernel to the other side. He got as far as the island before the lights

16

turned green. On either side of him cars roared into life, replicas frozen to the wheel. In a crowd, he crossed the final stretch.

At his approach the photo-booth bloomed into light. *Exposures Done in One Minute. Four Snaps for Two Bob.* The light went off.

John waited in a shop doorway out of the wet. He pushed the water from his hair with a flat hand until it squeaked. His levis clung coldly to his shins. 'Hurry up,' he said. Would the little extra, the little 'ow you say, register on film? It never had. 'Hurry up in there,' he said again, *sotto voce*, scene hater, 'as I've just lost my father, I was wondering if you could hurry up a bit see.'

The booth lit up for a fifth exposure, warranted, he deduced, by a further florin. More waiting. Shit. He thought of a hot drink and a sit down, won for bereavement. Carol would be the best and the nearest. Nice to have people making allowances — very pampering in an Eastern sort of way. He thought about the pampering in flamboyant fashion, revealing his lack of breeding and his early exposure to boys' comics. Wealth was to skate away the ragged boater with the poked up lid for a silky topper and astrakhan. Wealth was a dwarfing mound of banger and mash, bangers bounding like boomerangs from the waiter's tray; foaming regiments of pop and two cigars on a diamond pin. To this pre-pubertal picture he now added some sexual pampering, the mucky spoon lowered through the sprung lid of the boater and stirring in the brains.

The Richest Man in the World waddled into view heavy with pleasure, women's mouths glued to his erogenous zones like piglets… He would have to wear a black armband.

It was cold and damp in the shop doorway and stamping about only brought new areas of leg into contact with his wet jeans. He tried to penetrate the green booth curtains with a laser gaze. What unspeakable rites were being enacted within before the unshockable eye? The Most Beautiful Woman in the World proffering nude buttocks to the emplacement, winds the mushroom stool, adjustable for babies and gnomes, and clambers up above the front-face collars and ties to a pinnacle of bad taste. Here, she bares breasts that turn her into a group. John was best in life at interior monologues.

When the celluloid strip poked slowly out of the slot and slid down the chute into the rain-filled delivery tray, he galloped to intercept it and scan the subject matter. Silver strokes, graves and acutes sprang from his boots as he ran and he had to stutter on one foot to avoid whamming into the booth. He stood in the doorway and looked down at the strip in his hand. It featured a small boy in a bow tie. His hair was Brylcreemed flat to his head except for a pushed ridge in the front and a waterspout at the back. He looked like a ventriloquist's dummy. He wasn't even nude. John could see that lad was a unit in some grotesque family that held cheerfulness as a premium, and that saw the unit as a being a universally likely lad. John's face ached merely looking at the grin and he replaced the photo in the delivery tray.

The wait and the wetting spoiled John's litmus: the little extra did not manifest.

2

'I am sorry, John — you know that,' said Carol from the alcove, cheek pressed against the window-pane, eyes glissading down the sad slate rooftops to sadder asphalt. 'There's nothing I can say.'

John nodded and kept his face grave and composed while behind it he watched her reactions to his tidings. These were disappointing in a way. The same beautiful Pre-Raphaelite tristesse took the field, face lengthening, eyes writ large, mien droopy; the same expression, in fact, that he had observed floating over Byron, over Shelley, amongst woods'n fields. He had half-hoped for something special, kept under wraps perhaps and unfurled for the really big deals.

'We weren't very close,' he said. Cushioning fact.

'Would it help you to talk about it?'

He told her about the viewing in the morgue. He arranged it with facility into neat episodes, leaning heavily on literature and the movies for emotion, but limiting his palette to her range of empathy. He couldn't, however, resist the blade-straight exit into the rain from Hemingway; after all, he hadn't really stumbled away, eyes dazzled, in a cloak. The experience became a totality as he spoke until it ceased to exist except in these words, in this style, and his own unsounded feelings were buried alive. Still, he thought, her face warm now on his chest, inarticulate grief wouldn't do for her.

He held her away from him, held her hands and gave them a kindly chivvying little squeeze. 'Hey, come on kiddo. Ladies unmanned? You'll be lifting the seat next. Get me a nice cup of coffee.' And watched her obedient, rallying passage to the kitchen with a bidder's eye.

Sinking into her bed, he bore intact the image of her fashionable shoes retreating, plumply naked heels like bare, uncleft bottoms on pedestals. To stop this train of thought he forced his eyes to focus on his surroundings, the furnishings and fittings of Carol's familiar room. There was a lot of his history in the room. There were the shelves that he, cack-handed craftsman, had erected in two days of strain and congratulation, threatened now with a hundredweight of culture, some of which was his too. Really the room looked splendid, quite different from the rest of the house which was old, jaded and gloomy. He stared at the bright white walls, at the display of pressed, embossed ferns over the mantelpiece, anything to stop him thinking below the belt. Now he tried to midwife up a healthy remembrance posy for his father but drew only the Light programme and the little sticky sounds his schoolboy elbows made on the plastic tablecloth. Little enough for twenty years together. Anyway, the radio had gone off for poppa; light comedy, light music, soufflé serials; click — off. And the silence was balmy.

John sat up and reached for the carrier bag. He had already forgotten what he had signed for at the morgue. His hand shook a little as he plunged it into the neck and he wondered why people's things could upset when their death did not, gave that one up, and produced a silver watch on a long silver chain.

Carol, emerging from the kitchen with two pottery mugs saw him recumbent, Roman on one elbow, swinging the watch like a pendulum and gazing at it — she thought — like one facing the eternal questions. Tenderness flowed out from her to such beauty in bereavement.

'My father left me this,' he said. 'It doesn't work. His father gave it to him and he bequeathed it to me. My ancestors left me a stopped watch. Big symbol. It shouldn't have hands really but there you are.

He gave a quick effacing grin but it was too late. Carol had been upset. She put down the coffee and took the watch from him. 'You mustn't let yourself get bitter John. They gave what they had.' She ran her slender fingers over the cracked glass, over the scrolled silver back like a blind person familiarising, and suddenly John hated her, hated her for guessing wrong but more, an old hate for habitually touching things with her finger-tips as if everything was meant to arch beneath them. It was all he could do to stop himself from snatching the watch from her, and then the feeling passed.

'You can have it if you want. It's no good to me. Get it mended and wear it round your neck.'

She was shocked. The watch had been handled and consulted by his family for a hundred years, therefore it was of value. Couldn't he appreciate that? It had marched through the night from the dresser and hung, beating, below the heart at countless weddings and innumerable christenings and it was theirs and their children's now as earth is, for they had mixed their sweat and their lives with it.

'Do you know Dylan's poem "Do Not Go Gentle Into That Good Night"?' She raised her lovely dark eyes to his, willing his reply.

'"Rage, Rage Against the Dying of the Light". He always did. I preferred the Third. That in a way could stand as an emblem of our mutual disinterest.' Then, forced into declaration, covering up the crude uncaring pun with more words, he began: 'Listen Carol. He's dead and I don't feel a damn thing. I would if I could. Those who cry are the lucky ones. My father wasn't remotely interested in me — in fact, he wasn't interested or involved in anything. I'm not making this up. There are millions of people like him, people that God uses for crowd scenes. He was dead from the neck up. He occupied a certain space in the dining-room, displaced so many cubic feet of air and sometimes he made noises at me and I made noises back. There was no purpose or meaning to it then and there's certainly none now because he's dead. For me he was never any other way.' John realised to his surprise that in a spontaneous sort of way he was waving good-bye to her. Carol would never sit still for this lot. Perversely, he went on.

'You never meet him did you Carol? I get the feeling that you see him as a sort of DH Lawrence character — collar off, bony old calloused hands hanging between his knees as he sits at the fire. Sturdy old boots glowing red and then black again in the fire-light. Believe me, I'd have settled for that too. I'm not a snob you know. In reality my father was a turd. In every respect turd-like, and you can't get life-affirming on a turd. For a start he never had an opinion on anything — he believed that opinions went before a fall. He lived as anonymously as possible, blended with the wallpaper, but, and here's the nasty little paradox, he prided himself on his looks. He spent pounds on his hair alone. He had his double crown returfed and a parting dug…'

'Whatever he was, John, he was your father.' Carol sat on the edge of the bed and frowning, stroked the thick green pile of the blanket. The fading light from the street simplified her face into a pale, ethereal oval that seemed to hang in space, logical latitude eclipsed in the wash of black hair into the black mini-dress she had chosen for tragedy. None of it jelled, thought John, secretly gazing at the wistful girl with the sexy body, a fruity sundae with dream topping. Not that he could shout, Batman programmed to shrug, alike in a limbo of cancellation. A concealed zip snaked down the back of her dress, he noted.

'Labels and words,' he said irritably. 'Don't keep saying he was my father. I know he was my father. He was the cat's master too, and the factory's machine minder and the lavatory's most dramatic contributor. Why don't you pull some of them? He had a lot going for him. And now he's a stiff — his latest and greatest role. Sydney Jenkins, the Lord of the Flies.'

This was asking for trouble. He could see himself alone outside her door already, spurned zombie all washed up, but he could not stop sleepwalking towards that destination. The edges of his mind sniggered facetiously under the inflexible and liberating regime of this predestination. So why didn't she offer him the proverbial solace of her body? It would be very much Carol's style to balance father's end with hers, to get the old dam of pent-up feeling to break over her and then bathe in it for its spiritually cosmetic properties. But Carol spoke not a word.

'I suppose all the bloody diseased Jenkins line will turn out for the funeral,' he said, and sipped his coffee. She would not even look at him.

'He was lucky he wasn't run over,' he said provocatively but she wasn't biting. 'Because that would seem meaningless.'

Carol refused to enter into such a poltergeist spirit of things. 'Then again, it's a pity he wasn't murdered. That would have conferred importance on him, see. Sort of reassuring for the line.' He put out a hand to touch her but she shook him off with a movement like a shudder.

'You're a cold-hearted bastard,' she cried.

'Oh come on. I can't help it, can I? I've explained all that.'

Carol got up and stared out of the window into the darkening street. The roofs seemed to buckle silently into humps like some prehistoric armoured monster as she gazed through the streaming glass. Her world was reeling. As the tears ran down her cheeks, she traced the moving rain drops with her finger, and felt emotion and nature epiphanise into one.

'Just go away.'

Again the edges of his mind curled up like burning paper. 'I doubt if you'll put all this down to shock?' Inside, he was alive with laughter. His stomach fluttered and he thought he was going to be sick. He took out the strip of photos and laid them on the bed. Not much of a sacrifice really. The whole photo album idea had gone stale. He had nurtured the embryo idea through the waiting months of gestation to its brilliant birth; the strange longing to see a warp in life other than his nature, a woof other than Spot. One morning two years ago he had felt a tiny boot in his swollen lobes and before he could boil a kettle there it was, all shining and utterly absorbing. So he took the photos. None of them showed anything significant: the same unchanging face looked out of the album, coarsened by turkey, brutalised by pud, earthbound. Life had written nothing on those features. When he looked at the idea he was struck by its idiot, mongoloid aspect. John Jenkins, Columbus of the uterus. Old Carol could have them.

She heard the door quietly close behind him, a rush of air on her skin. Still crying she went instinctively to the typewriter as John had gone to the photo booth, and just as hopelessly tried to record her communion with sorrow. When she was happy the sun shone on her, when it rained she cried, herself a French reflexive verb. Carol was emotionally labile, balanced on a knife edge between tears and joy, though not as often as she could have wished. She was still a Luxemburg DJ compared to Werther and Byron, but she was working at it. And she worked at it now, blanket-bombing the sheet, the room filled with the metallic clacking of artistic creation, the little typewriter bell tolling the knell of passing day.

3

John awoke in his bedroom at midday wondering what unprecedented and genial spirit had visited his father, staying his rudely poking finger at 7.30am. Then he remembered that his father was dead. He lay there wondering if he cared today because today was a new day, and grief and loss might operate in the nature of a yeast. He tried all the corks. Firm as ever. He didn't care today either.

He tried Carol next. There was a faint and sluggish stirring which pleased him no end. He had actually felt a twinge, a real organic twinge, without shaking the bottle. He gave himself up to a contemplation of the silver lining; by next Saturday he might feel even worse. He lay flat on his back caring away, his eyes gliding easily over the familiarities of his room.

Should he write to her now on the strength of his expectation of grief? Would that be jumping the gun? The warmth of the bed sapped his resolve. He sneezed directly up into the air and felt the spray patter back deliciously on his face. It occurred to him suddenly that she may consider the affair off, and already be roistering around looking for a replacement. That almost flushed him from his thicket. John's better half remonstrated with him in the sensible didactic tone of a pipe-smoker; strike while the iron is hot, a stitch in time, stuff like that. This better half was essentially a knock about figure, and John knew that one sidelong glance from him was enough to deflate the half down to a smirky accomplice. They had both been at it for a long time.

The conflict, to overstate this rubber sabre-rattling, was resolved by John's bladder. It needed emptying. He arose with a sigh, emptied it, and returning saw, incredibly, paper and pen in meaningful juxtaposition on his desk. He sat down and picked up the pen.

'Dear Carol,' he wrote, and then paused reflectively. He nibbled at the collar of his pyjamas. Had they drawn the ultimate curtain of intimacy, and there behind the arras pledged sacred vows as they commingled, gasping, clasping, to the very quick of their being? No, they hadn't. Still, that was hardly her fault.

'My dear Carol,' he wrote, and paused again. John Jenkins the last of the big pausers. He wondered if she would notice the new possessiveness and reinstate him. Should he underline it? He decided against; that would be as juvenile as writing SWALK on the back of the envelope. It was easy for him to write a moving letter, the naked soul dragging its poor lamed presence across the page. Too easy. Six four-foot stacks of novels stood against his bedroom wall; all the novelists that the sociologists predicted for him, as inexorably as 'A' follows 'O'. John had read them all and he could serve up a piping dollop of Kafka, Dostoevsky, Sartre and West that would have her crying on her loom for weeks. So what? What sort of relationship was he going to offer her? That was the problem.

John read it through. 'My dear Carol': all right so far. He took a new sheet, and resting his hand on the blotter wrote this out again for neatness. Really, he was becoming thoroughly disenchanted with his twinge of twenty minutes ago. If he had to go through this lot for a twinge, a flutter might scupper. Supposing he had loved his father, the no-mark, and mourned his passing? God, that would be rough. Holy smoke no joke. No wonder Mrs Next-Door — Mrs Plume — had belted hell out of the door at 2am last night to see if he was all right and to offer, could we have the cup back, her condolences. She should have offered herself with hubby Plume as afters. What Mrs Plume had said was:

'And so sudden — no warning at all.'

To which John in high spirits had replied: 'It would have been unreasonable to expect one as he fell into the estuary.'

This was hopeless. He stared at the paper in vexation for several seconds, rattling the pen against his teeth. Then hastily he bent again to the task and before he had quite gathered his thoughts the pen had written, as if possessed of some private and professional obligation of its own: 'I hope you are well.'

John jumped up and ran to the lavatory with the letter balled in his fist, hurled it into the pan and sent it speeding to some Lethe with a pull of the chain. Sod the letter. He went into the bathroom and ran the bath.

As it filled, his thoughts began to wander along the unsequestered path of sex. A myriad suspenders and brassieres broke cover and scattered in panic at his passing. He thought of Carol's eager young thrusters and he thought of Carol's biteable buttocks. Vacantly, he unbuttoned his pyjama jacket and pulled the ripcord that sent his trousers bailing out over his feet. Steam rose from the bath. Why hadn't he leapt upon her? Had she not by woman's art, on bed and bower, hinted at the whirling vortex behind her underwear? A score of eager hands surged skywards: 'Please sir, me sir!' Indeed she had.

In a dream he bent to turn off the taps. Gazing at the plug, a wobbly blob, he tried to divine this whirling vortex behind her underwear. He boggled before the mysterious panel, through lack of information. The taps dripped musically into the bath. Perhaps scientific method was the answer; collect your information, assess it, draw a conclusion. Carol's eyebrows! On the hypothesis that the study of a single tree would indicate the nature of the forest, John tweezed an eyebrow from memory and examined it. He could rely on his specimen. Carol's face remained an outpost of truth, unplucked, unpruned; Diana of the Uplands. He concluded that Carol was splendidly endowed with maidenfern. This scientific method was a bugger, he mused, looking down at himself.

The Richest Man in the World sat in his director's chair in the boardroom, intermittently visible around the bobbing woman astride his lap. His commands were incoherent; his senses plethoric with tongues and tremors. His lowliest employee lived for the hour when the wing-less bluebottle would sprint ticklingly around his helmet, a lighthouse in the bath.

John's bath was cold and accusing. Later, washed, shaved, combed and clad the idea took root that he must institute a new regime of early rising, constructive thought and hygienic movements, the latter perhaps in the park. Not that this idea was new; he had, in his head, an auto-change device for new leaves to eliminate wasted effort. Still, perhaps this time he would be able to stick to it. Perhaps his father's death would lend impetus to his resolve. There was no reason why the passing should go to waste when it could be useful as a calendar mark.

He flung open all the windows in his bedroom and took deep lungfuls of fresh air. He looked out at the street. Off-white net curtains as far as the eye could see, and in the next-door garden a few plastic soldiers sat in the dirt waiting for dinner to finish. A few gardens up, a To Let sign like a petrified flag.

John stripped down his bed, shook everything, put down clean sheets and remade it. Then he rounded up all the dirty socks, shirts and pants and stuffed them into a pink polythene bag for the laundry. All this was the flip-side of the leaf. Previously he had let his dirty stuff lie fallow for a while in the corner before wearing it again. Sitting on his bed extracting cuff-links, he devised a tariff of fines for his laundry: pants — skid-marked — one shilling: flare-pathed — one and three. As an added deterrent against recidivism he could send an accompanying letter:

Dear Laundry,
I enclose the following for your rhubarb. Use visor and tongs.
Yours, proud but ill-wiped, John Jenkins.

Like a coda came the memory of the manure races of his childhood. His father had pushed the coal shovel into his hand and he had raced, an Olympic relay-runner, out into the street to reach the pile of steaming manure left by Prince Philip, horse to FP Philip, Castoffs, before his panting neighbours. Success in this field really got through to his father. He would stand in the doorway laughing at the others as John ran home with his piping prize. Yes, the old man had loved the shitrace. Well, John sighed, *recherchez*-wise Proust hadn't got a lot to worry about.

He dabbed at a few dusty surfaces with a sock and then put that in with the rest of the washing. He emptied the ashtray out of the window. On the landing he remembered his father's room; his ex-father's ex-room.

He opened the door and went in. Naturally nothing had changed, nothing here was disturbed by the passing of the occupant. That was the way it went with inanimates, thought John, and that made it unanimous.

'You didn't make the bed,' he said into the pressing silence. He patted the foot of the bed to locate the hot-water bottle and found it sagging obscenely in a fold of sheet. It slid out and slapped onto the lino, cold and rubbery. He could hardly bear to touch it. When he pulled back the sheets he was suddenly aware of that same unveiling, the empty bed a more nauseating mansion for death, of his father's cold and tallow body in the morgue. It was an effort to go on, to strip the bed and roll back the mattress and impose a final order on the flotsam that remained of his father's life. He made himself see the job through, sorting out the clothes in the wardrobe, the shirts and socks and underwear in the chest of drawers, poking through the pockets and finding nothing. He had got the whole worthless bundle dragged out and into his own room when the bell went. Arthur stood on the porch.

'I just dropped round to say I heard about your dad.' He gave a crippling squeeze to John's shoulder and barged into the hall. John despondently followed him into the kitchen. Arthur bored him stiff; brute force personified. He was always disappointed that Arthur used doors, having simplified him down to Arthur-shaped egress holes in brickwork, a monolith avid over cow-pie. Arthur was sitting on a flimsy kitchen chair like a samurai. His fists rested loose on his knees and a hard bulge of belly and chest rose into the broad red warhead.

'Fooking sad,' he said.

'Here today and gone tomorrow,' replied John, feeding him a line he felt he could handle.

'Gone today,' said Arthur profoundly, reminding John that he had been hanging around with undergraduates. The university socialists had practically adopted him, and now he sat on every committee and on every platform, adding the weight and dignity of his wellies to their pale face dialectics. He had never been bashful; now he was unstoppable, talking and everything.

'Nice of you to come.' John always laid down a broad yellow stripe for the wellies to walk on and wished again that he wasn't taller than Arthur. Arthur had been known to resent height in others; clearly they were trying to make something of it. Still taller ten year-old John Jenkins had hit C above C in the playground under the blows of the cub-capped crusher; neither had changed.

'I had the day off, so I come.'

As he filled the kettle and placed it on the gas, John thought how Arthur's conversation tended towards the terminal. Perhaps because silence didn't bother him.

'Still got that sissy haircut then.'

'Hee hee,' laughed John at this fustian shaft.

'Haven't seen you at Bell's meetings then.'

A rallying visit like this could last all day, depending really on John's degree of supinity. Horrible when things were up to him.

'You go, do you Arthur?'

'Oh I go. I'm on the committee. I'm a big wheel.' His deprecatory sniff downgraded the machine only. John was quick to take his cue.

'You're the only bloody worker there,' he said ardently and thought of Colin Bell's leather wrist-brace.

'Aye,' said Arthur. 'There's not one on them'ud last five minutes down the dock. Any road — I don't need them but they do need me. So that's alreet.' He drank his tea boiling with great wet schlurps. John could see that Arthur was beginning to believe the politicians' picture of himself. He should get his arms tattooed: *I Love Splosh*: something like that.

'You don't want to keep it all bottled up you know,' said Arthur after a long noisy silence.

'The grief?' John was startled into an incautious reply.

'Aye. It must out somewhere. That's your trouble—' he leaned creakingly forward and jabbed an iron digit into John's side —'you Intellectuals.'

John was sure something had come loose.

'What would you do if your old man died?' he painfully asked.

The huge red fist crashed onto the table. Shock waves caused a scurrying among the piled crockery on the draining board and one plate fell down and broke. John tried not to flick his eyes at the sink. When someone clears the way for a statement in that fashion, the audience is expected to pay attention; he'd read around.

'I'd run a-fooking-mok!'

There it was: clear: direct: stupid.

'Best thing,' said John.

'Only thing.'

Silence fell. It was Arthur's silence, put there for John to assimilate the message. He used it as respectfully as if it were his own, in which to think unconnected and irrelevant thoughts. 'The day our Binkie died I put four blokes away,' said Arthur.

This struck John as terrifically yielding of interpretation. Arthur put blokes away like a squirrel puts away nuts. Had

Arthur put these blokes to death, tribal ritualistic, Golden Bough, to accompany Binkie on her journey to that bourne of shades, one to carry her cushion, one her saucer…?

'You remember our Binkie.'

'Oh yes.' John started guiltily. 'Binkie was a helluva good — old Binks. Yes sir!'

'Used to watch you going to school with yer bloody great bag of books. Workin' lad getting on, I used to say.'

'I remember,' said John, blank on Binkie — what was the blasted thing?

'Had a crush on you, you know.'

He's taken leave, John thought. It had to be a female then, for Arthur would never admit to even an aberrant cat under his roof. An 'twere a blasted cat. Without thinking, John took a flier. 'We used to wave at each other in the mornings,' he blurted and then flushed crimson. Arthur was staring at him, lifting his great brows on their red cartilage like masonry on a stone face. Driven on in panic he said: 'I'd just wave — like this — Coo-oo, and she'd just wave her old — ha ha appendage.'

'You're trying to come it, shag.' The brows descended. Four had been put away already.

'I don't know what you mean, Arthur. Really.'

'You know fooking well what I mean. How could a fooking budgie wave at you, you daft twit.'

There it was. And there he was with egg on his face.

'Seemed to wave, Arthur. Trick of the light perhaps. Eyestrain ha ha — you know us Intellectuals. The eyes go first and then the pectorals.'

'You'd bloody well forgotten, who Binkie was, hadn't you? Own up. I could see that a mile off.'

'Well, just for a moment. I hadn't thought of old —'

'And you thought I was going to thump you, you daft sod. D'you think I don't know as how you've more on your mind than our fooking Binkie?'

'I didn't want to hurt your feelings,' John offered.

'It was bloody years ago man.' Arthur yawned happily, stretching his arms and turning his wrists back and forth as if pumping the air out of his mouth. John felt obliged to watch so large a gesture. He hoped Arthur was off. He needed this solace like a hole in the head: but then Arthur ran a hole in the head business. Then suddenly, skittishly, John was off the ropes slugging.

'My father had a parrot,' he said with a sad expression.

Arthur made his mouth smaller.

'He was stationed in India in the war, miles from anywhere. All the men were yawning their heads off with nothing to do, my father said. There was a sort of craze for parrots on the camp — you know the kind of thing, Arthur.'

Arthur nodded, commanded by the serious manner. He fidgeted with the knife and fork on the table, moving them farther apart as if in anticipation of a larger meal.

'My father said it was a Green Hell in the barracks with all those parrots singing and swearing at once like under-oiled machinery. There was a big Irish rifleman in my father's regiment who had a parrot called Tone — after Wolfe Tone the Hebrew cyclist. Tone could say anything. He was a genius. While all the other parrots were stumbling through beak-sullying epithets and pitiful drinking songs, Tone would be reciting Robert Emmet's epitaph. Everyone got very tensed up and competitive about it. You know how it is Arthur, you want the best for your parrot. My father said he used to blow into the neck feathers to check that his parrot's ears hadn't got bunged up with seed husks or a stray quill. No-one could account for Tone's fantastic memory. They began to watch Tone and the Irishman to see if anything special passed between them but nothing ever did. It was weeks before they found out.

'One evening the Irishman and the parrot crossed the long hot room and disappeared through the door. My father watched them walking over the parade ground, one with long strides, one with short, side by side.'

At this point Arthur shifted uneasily on the kitchen chair and began to moon over his fists. He had to listen to this crap because it belonged to John's freshly corpsed father; respect demanded too that it was not funny. A heavy yoke.

John fixed blocky Arthur with a sombre eye and continued. He had enjoyed the story so far and he wondered interestedly what his father would discover.

'My father followed them, using available shadows and avoiding any twigs, until his quarries came to a halt just out of camp limits, by a well. As you know, Arthur, India abounded with wells at that time. From behind a convenient rock he saw the Irishman take a length of string and a book from his shirt pocket, tie the string around the parrot like a truss and hold the other end while the parrot jumped forward and down, disappearing from view. The Irishman began to read from his book, projecting his voice down the well.'

John was amazed that Arthur sat still for this lot. 'My father said it was very eerie. Picture it, Arthur. A deserted and parched wilderness at dusk — a lonely figure in shorts erect beside a well — silence swathing the world like a giant dhoti.'

'Pretty rum,' Arthur conceded, yawning with his mouth closed. 'Well, I'd better be…' He slapped his knees and prised his mighty buttocks from the seat.

'It was one of the last stories my father told me before he…' said John. Arthur settled dourly back.

'My father said that parrots are shallow creatures and easily distracted. They lack, as a brood, concentration. Now you isolate your average parrot, Arthur; suspend him on a string down a well and drop your words down singly like pearls. Get my meaning? Anyway my father told the others what he'd seen and they all drifted out of the barracks in twos and threes and assembled at the well. They didn't really have a plan — it just happened. They sat swigging beer and laughing about the secret of Tone's wizardry. After a bit one of them went and pissed down the well and then they all followed, emptying their bladders in glittering and hilarious curves onto the moon's reflection. The water level rose a foot and a half and the next night Tone was *drowned*.

'When the Irishman hauled up his bird it was all sodden and stiff. That great beak was stilled, Arthur. Binkie all over again.

John looked at Arthur, drawing his restless gaze into his own damp eyes.

'Fooking sad,' said Arthur and shook his head as if to clear it. He stood up. 'You want to take your mind off things man. Go down town. Get yourself fixed up with a bit of crumpet, eh?' He surged potently with his fist in the air, but his expression held a wilted quality. 'A bit of the other, eh?' And he blundered off.

4

John caught a bus, sat on it to the terminus and then got one going the other way. He jumped off where he had started from. All the way he had said to himself the names of the shops they were passing. Coming back he counted them. Then he went into the King's Head and drank six pints with six whiskies as chasers. He was depressed. Alcohol is a great panacea and soon he felt physically dislocated and depressed.

He recognised a face. 'Joseph,' he said. He was not reading; he just knew it was Joseph. He felt very warm and friendly towards Joseph although sometimes he bored him stiff. A big smile swilled around his face. Joseph smiled back because he liked to smile in public. They stood facing each other like heliograph experts.

'Hi Johnny,' said Joseph, reluctantly sheathing his smile. Joseph counted John as one of his friends and Joseph thought of his friends as family, cursing and cheating them as he did his kith, but never deserting them. He copied little bits of all his friends, their mannerisms, their opinions, and produced these before their eyes with a flourish like a team cup. Some people exchange comment about shared experiences, and this is the basis of their friendship: Joseph merely skipped the external stimulus and shared a common brain. His friends knew his sources and he knew that they knew and believed they would be flattered. They knew that he knew that they knew and wondered why he didn't feel a prick. John liked him.

They sat at one of the stone-topped tables. Every time John put his elbow on the table it rocked about and beer slopped out of the glasses because one of the legs was too short. He bent and stared under the table. A folded cigarette packet was wedged under the short leg, redressing about a quarter of an inch of the three inch gap. He sat up. His head felt like an egg-timer after this movement. Sound burst about his ears like a handful of flung coins. John put his elbow on the table and it rocked again, spilling the beer. He was behaving like a lobotomy case.

'Let's get out of here,' he said, and Joseph raised his glass, throat gulping and made little chops in the air to signify assent.

'I never liked this pubic house,' he said, reissuing an old release — John's property. They barged through the crowd and out into the fresh air of the alley. They urinated in unison under the moon, backs arched back like two saxophone players, and the silvered notes plashed upon their shadows. Joseph felt very close to John and his breast ached with friendship and family feeling. He did not give voice to it because John hadn't buttoned up and he feared he might be misunderstood.

'Come on, I'll teach you snooker,' he said.

'I'm too pissed,' said John. 'How far is it?' He lurched against the wall.

'Just up the road. Not far.'

'Bags I Paul Newman.' John fell back against the wall screaming with laughter.

The pool hall was an old building, the air of a men's hostel clinging to it with the tenacity of a tramp's fart. The tables were threadbare and the rims were pocked with the burns of generations of unattended cigarettes. Little groups of men stood around watching the games from under cloth caps. Joseph always thought of the hall and the clientele as Fabian and this pleased him; the game itself he treated as a family craft, the wholesome fruit of class solidarity. He shouted greetings to various loungers —'great blokes'— and steered John to an empty table.

'Now this is the idea of the game,' he said, and explained.

John's head reeled. He couldn't seem to concentrate on what Joseph was saying but desperately stared at his opening and closing mouth. 'I'll watch you for a bit and pick it up,' he said.

'No no,' Joseph was insistent. 'You can't learn like that — you have to play. Come, on, you can start.'

Gripping the cue John bent over the table and sighted at the coloured balls prancing on the green like morris dancers. He missed everything except the cushions and his ball battered around for a while and slowly came to rest.

'Right, my go,' said Joseph and potted a bail. He strode around the table diminishing the balls in a series of sharp, efficient clicks. He had his jacket off, his hat over his eyes and he felt generally like the original hustler. 'Fifty,' he said, 'red, six pocket.' Click — the red ball joined the bulging pocket with a clatter, the cigarette arced up, glowed, descended. 'You can't learn by watching, John. You have to get into the thick of it mate. Sixty. Green, four pocket.'

'Yes,' said John, and chalked his thumb.

The match lasted twenty-five minutes. Joseph scored one hundred and twenty and then declared. John idled against the wall and tried not to fall down.

'Let's go to my pad and hear some records,' said victor Joseph.

'I'd better go home now,' said John. 'Is it far?'

'Just up the road. Not far.'

Joseph's pad was very comfortable, Joseph thought. John thought so too tonight, but he was pissed. He slumped into an externally sprung armchair.

'I'll make you a black coffee,' said Joseph, making a chef's 'O' with finger and thumb. He had no milk. The machine outside had broken — he had hurt his foot kicking it and had retired in a flurry of spit and gristle with the toe of one boot bent up like a Turk's. Joseph always bought boots with Cuban heels to give height and two sizes too big to make his trousers look tighter. His trousers were sprayed on now but the mould beneath was short and stubby enough to resemble wheels.

John's rolling eyes slid over the familiar décor. The wall behind the gramophone was covered with record sleeves neatly spaced several inches apart. Where the wallpaper showed between it was Laocoön and floral. It gave John the impression that the wall was bulging out toward him, each eruption represented by a straining black face with a saxophone in it. Well, now there was nothing to stop him from altering his place to suit himself, except, of course, the unbearable responsibility involved in pleasing himself.

'Sorry to hear about your Dad,' said Joseph, offering moist eyes like the grapes of a hospital visit, an enamel mug of black coffee in each hand.

'Don't worry about it. We never got on.'

Joseph would have envied that in the James Dean era, had he not been twelve at that time, but he was now in the blood and brotherhood grip of Marx and Ma Joad. So he said, coming right out with it, 'Still...'

'Forget it.' John closed his eyes and leaned back to listen to the record, letting the cycles of tension and resolution fill his mind. He really listened in to it, anticipating the huge squalling sounds of Coltrane, vintage '65. He heard the drummer break out the cymbal under the soprano, splintering like ice under the shrill skater, ice flaring behind the skater no way out but ahead, moving always ahead of it. He heard the strain in it, tendons sticking through the sound, fibrous sounds of throat prolapsed into horn, strain in the hissing fragments that fell back like shavings, snapped and curled in the rush of passing. When it was over John saw that the skater drowning in spinning black swirls was an LP needle now clicking idiotically back and forth in the centre. You brought your own gerunds, he thought, and you left your ear at home. You took a great thing and you made it small enough to handle.

'That,' shouted Joseph, putting his hands on his head to keep it on, 'is one fat panic!'

'You've been at the sleeve notes again.'

A loud, hysterical knocking at the door presaged complaints. It was the girl from the next room. 'Turn that bloody racket down or I'll call...'

'Racket! That's music — you wouldn't know music from a hole in the wall,' Joseph shouted.

'You turn it down!'

'You get stuffed.' As he slammed the door, Joseph licked his forefinger and drew a phantom score in the air. He felt very pleased with himself tonight. 'She fancies me, you know. Stupid gash.'

'Lay God's voice on her,' said John.

'Rollins.'

They played Rollins and Lester and Griffin and Bean and then switched to alto as a chaser and played Bird and Ornette. They became very hot.

'Will you get a gram now — you know?' Joseph made a vague gesture indicating the demise of Mr Jenkins, his planting elsewhere and the subsequent pastures of freedom: an inclusive gesture.

'I'd never go out,' John replied.

'Well, you can always hear mine. Oh yeah, thanks for the Emitex Anti-Magnetic Anti-Static Eeziwipe Record Cleaner.'

'Don't mention it.'

Comradeship hung in the air like cigar smoke. They got out the old jokes because the old jokes were the best; they kept the squares off the stand like the complex chord changes on the record player.

'You think Ayler is putting us on?'

'No.'

'Cecil Taylor?'

'No.'

'Brubeck?'

'He's gone too far.'

There was a lot of that, of thigh-slap and rib-tickle, before the drink wore off. It was Joseph who introduced a note of sobriety, returning, as if to ennoble the fun with brotherly feeling, to the subject of John's father. 'Don't you miss him at all?' he earnestly asked.

'Who?'

'Well, your father, of course. I thought you looked pretty low in the pub.'

'Not about that.'

'Something else?'

'It would be.'

Not put off, Joseph investigated further. 'Would it help you to talk about it? It helps to talk to a mate. You know, it sort of straightens things out — gives you perspective. You don't want to bottle it up inside you because that's dangerous for your personality — gives you —'

'You mean you want to know what's on my mind?' said John, remembering Arthur.

'Of course I don't! I don't personally give a shit what's on your mind. I was only thinking of you.' Joseph hoisted his eyebrows into his hat to show complete lack of interest in the matter. He went and lay on his bed under the shelf of sociology books with titles like The Aged Poor in Action. He couldn't afford to waste time on silly sods. He worked a cigarette out of his pocket without disclosing his source, an expertise he possessed in many fields, and stuck it into the corner of his mouth. He tried his pockets for a light, but in vain. By the time he had rolled off the bed and come back from the kitchen with a match he had forgotten that he was annoyed. His temperament and his movements were alike mercurial. A pinball machine, lighting up in all directions as the influences were fed into the slot.

'Johnnie?' he said.

'Yes?' John opened his eyes wearily.

'I've got a problem.

'*You've* got a problem!'

Joseph surged over this and pulled up a chair. He sat on it, back to front, arms dangling over the back, as over a garden fence.

'This really bugs me, Johnnie. It gets so I can't sleep nights.'

He extended his packet of cigarettes to John.

'It must be worse than Hamlet's,' said John, eyes firing amazed tracers into the packet.

'Do you worry about, you know, sex? I mean, I've thought about it till its really hung me up the most. I can't sleep—'

'You said.'

'Man, I can't even hear my records sometimes!'

'When the gram's on?'

'Of course when the bleeding gram is on. You think I'm a bleeding idiot or something? I've got to talk to you about it — after all, that's what mates are for.'

'Sure I worry. We all worry. Everybody worries. In fact it's a load of worry all round. Everybody wants to be a stud: nobody is. Except me, of course.

'Yes dad, but what do you worry about? You know, which bit?' Joseph hoped that John's worry was worse, more unmanning, than his, but he kept this from himself.

'I suppose I ought to worry because I don't want to do it. Not with either sex. It could be that I have a fear and hatred of children, that I carry over into the act — anyway that's what Carol says. Frequently. She says I'm an introvert. Worry all the time about the meaninglessness of life. Four generations of bobbing arses produced nothing but a line of mobile afterbirths, but its going to stop with me. Carol can tell you more about it, ask her.'

'Yes, that's a valid point of view.' Joseph was very intrigued by these disclosures, but nevertheless eager now to get on with his own. 'I worry about that all the time. Like what a bleeding washout the world is and how there's no hope and that. But of course you have to take the rough with the smooth.' John quietly boggled at the transition from Trotsky to Stalin. The lack of bloodshed never ceased to appal him. There was clearly a great chasm between them.

Joseph lobbed a pea into this chasm for John to cross. 'Well you know. No time, no time, dig everything.' He continued impatiently, 'I want kids, of course. I'm a great Admirer of my Father. He's — you dig — a Great Man and a Truly Warm Person. I want to be like him. I want my kids to look up to me, ask my advice.' He laid his stubby hand on his breast. 'My problem is really the flipside of yours, see. I worry that I won't be able to produce a family and worrying about that is putting the mockers on me performance. I got this trauma. Also, I don't get to test me performance in this crummy town. Worst of all is this frustration.' He stopped talking, and John understood that it was all up to him. He could see where he had gone wrong. He never should have let loose with Carol's diagnosis. Joseph had misunderstood, had assumed that John was giving him his all and had followed suit. Of course, he couldn't know that John was willing to throw in his father, his unremembered mother, a posy of used Kleenex, a child's garden of faeces, everything in fact that could be staked with words, add his marker, go home in a barrel with bracers and still be ahead. Because none of it was important.

'It's the mojo, Joseph. Chicken claws and effigies and pointing bones. That's why you can't get your leg over.'

A sudden and startling noise above cut him short.

'Christ!' John cried, half starting from his chair. 'What the hell is that?'

'It's all right,' shouted Joseph in an attempt to surf casually over the din. 'Go on about the mojo.'

'What the hell is that noise?'

'That rattling?' Joseph indicated the ceiling: useless farting against thunder.

'It's the only rattling we have.'

Joseph, shrugged uncomfortably. 'Probably the bloke upstairs.

'What's he doing, dying?'

'I don't know, do I? Ain't got X-ray eyes, have I?'

The noise rose to a crescendo and then stopped as abruptly as it had started, leaving Joseph bawling his rhetorical questions into a silent room.

'Anyway it's stopped,' he added, quieter. 'Go on about the

mojo.' John stared at him. Between hat and button-down he was crimson. Joseph was blushing! John was so startled that he acquiesced but his mind was not on the story.

'The mojo,' he said flatly. 'Yes. The ladies are afraid.'

'Uh huh, uh huh, I gotcha,' urged Joseph, posed like the Boyhood of Raleigh.

'Feature a man, Joseph, who has all his wires crossed. He's been conditioned perhaps — or just come out of scarlet fever.'

'Or mumps.'

'Yes or mumps. Mumps can be a bugger in adulthood. A swan can break your arm with a single blow of its wing. Anyway. This man sees a woman. She sees him. They are attracted. They go back to her place and she changes into something more comfortable. They embrace. They fall to the couch —'

John saw the light fixture jerk back and forth and up and down in a grotesque dance.

'What happened then,' screamed Joseph, trying vainly to run a scream and a twinkle in harness.

John pointed to the jerking light. 'He'll be through the ceiling in a minute!'

Joseph cupped his hands to his mouth like a megaphone: 'Go on with the story.'

At that moment a huge golden 800 watt light bulb lit up in John's head: it had *Idea* written in it and little lines radiated from the bulb. The noise was copulation. Or at least, and most important, Joseph thought it was. That was why he was blatting about like a blocked moth trying to keep him from the 800 watt light bulb. Obviously he was embarrassed by the speed and frequency of the performance above: more, he was afraid that it was normal: most, he was afraid that John would say it was.

The noise stopped.

'They fell to the couch?' said Joseph. Implored Joseph.

'Okay.' John shrugged. 'He begins to make love to her but his wires are crossed.'

'He's all hung up.'

'Yes. He listens to her neck, her breasts, her roseate halos. His ears begin to burn. He sniffs her parted lips. As his fever mounts a nasal hair protrudes. French sniffing now. He tastes her navel — quite nice in passing, but his drive is all towards One Thing. He parts her thighs. Now he transfixes her with a long, virile, penetrating stare. He looks away. He stares again. Stares mount into glances, quicker and quicker, quiff tossing. Now he's glimpsing — glimpse, glimpse, glimpse — then the final agonising, delicious blink. The man is satiated and he slumps on to the carpet. His nerveless fingers release the album of Eartha Kitt.'

'Does the woman like it? I mean, how can she pick up on this stuff?' As he waited tensely for the noise to recommence, Joseph tried to engage all of John's attention, scoop him up and enfeoff him, deaf to his environment until the final good night.

'No, she doesn't. That's the point. It's queers like that who stop men like you from getting their rights. They put a mojo on you. Now, that lady would think twice before she offered another bloke in.'

Joseph nodded vigorously. 'Could be, could be.'

'I thought I'd tell you straight rather than have you learn about it in some dirty furtive…'

The noise started again.

John put on his coat and prepared to leave, his host unquestioningly greasing his path.

'See ya tomorrow,' screamed Joseph into his ear, making him squeeze up his shoulder and bare his teeth.

John knocked quietly on the door upstairs. He felt his visit justified, sanctified even by his kindly restraint below. A middle-aged man in pyjamas and socks appeared.

'What is that noise?' asked John.

'Dynamo,' said the man.

'Thank you,' said John, running down the stairs, tip-toeing past Joseph's door, laughing like a drain.

5

Dr Ostbahn put his head around the door. The waiting-room was almost empty. A plain-looking girl sat stiffly in the corner seat, flicking nervously through an ancient *Punch* magazine. By the empty fireplace a young man sat, doing nothing.

'Next please,' the doctor said in his heavy German accent. He went back into his surgery and sat in the padded swivel chair. It had been a long day. They were all long now. He was old and his fat white hands were blotched with brown marks. He pulled out his old-fashioned watch; eight-thirty. Soon he could turn off the lights and go home. He read the inscription on the watch for the umpteenth time: *Eine festes Burg ist unser Gott*. Heidelberg, 1920. Once he had replaced it in his waistcoat he could never remember if he had just read the inscription or merely seen it in his mind; time was fleeting, God was a rock. He yawned with his mouth shut. His nostrils bulged wide and tears came into his eyes.

There was a knock on his door.

'Come in,' he said.

The girl came into the surgery awkwardly clutching a big black handbag. Her shoes squeaked on the ancient lino. She sat very straight on the chair, feet together, the bag in her lap. It was easy to see what was on her mind; no wedding ring, last in the surgery. But the doctor knew instinctively, without studying behaviour patterns. '*Wichtig*': important: pregnant. The word in German was very apt. She carried her importance about her like a nimbus and could no more elude it than Peter Pan his nailed-on shadow. She sat very upright on the chair like an exclamation mark.

Now the eternal pattern of question and answer must begin. Always the same, always the same. He suppressed another yawn.

'Well, Miss —?' he said.

'Miss Smith.' She didn't look up. Her fingers played nervously with the clasp of the handbag, and when it sprang open she rummaged around inside it.

'But of course. Miss Smith.' He smiled ironically. 'What seems to be the trouble?'

The girl placed the bag, half-open, on the floor beside her chair. She looked at him.

'I'm pregnant Dr Ostbahn.' The voice, like the gaze, was surprisingly direct — almost a challenge. Her lips came together tightly, with finality. She had passed the ball to him and now it was his turn.

'Ah. So you are going to have a baby.'

He knew that his reply was meaningless and he felt himself slip into the manner of a much older, much more ingenuous man. It was his habitual refuge, a putting on of spectacles before a fight.

'No. I said I was pregnant.' She ignored his infirmity.

Again he tried to guide the conversation into its proper channels, entrenching himself more firmly as the doddery, bespectacled alien for whom allowances have to be made.

'My dear, all women feel depression at some stage in pregnancy. It is natural. The back aches and the clothes do not fit. In the morning there is often sickness, nausea. Little things irritate. It is an irony that patience comes only with age.' The doctor leaned back and linked his fingers over his chest. 'When you are as old as me you will realise this. You cannot change nature. If you are pregnant you will have your baby. You can do nothing but wait.'

'I can get rid of it, can't I?' She smiled slightly.

'You are not married. Will the father stand by you?'

'I don't know who he is.'

'Ah, Youth, Youth.' He shook his head sadly. 'Never a thought for the morrow. But you must —'

'Will you help me get rid of it or not?' She sat tensely on the chair as if a refusal would send her instantly striding to the door.

Dr Ostbahn felt hustled, crowded into a coroner. Protocol had been trampled underfoot and the consultation had not progressed along his lines at all. He always did the job in the end, but first he had to hear the desperation, the pleading and the gratitude to stifle the remains of his professional conscience. He looked around his surgery. Everything was second-rate and threadbare. One of the castors on the couch had broken off. Last year's copies of Lancet lay unopened on the window-sill. Thirty years ago he would have thrown her and her brazen demands out of his surgery. Thirty years ago. Before the compromises and evasions and the all-pervading tiredness had rotted the fibres of his life like a crawling malignant disease.

'How late are you?' he wearily asked.

'A month.'

'You are sure of that?'

'Yes.'

'I will not touch your case if you are more. You understand? I am a doctor not an abortionist.' His irritation was beginning to show. He wanted to get it over with and get rid of this patient. She stared at him, straight-backed and immobile.

'How much?' she said.

'First I must examine you. We will talk money afterwards.'

'No. First I must know how much you charge, Dr Ostbahn.'

A very business-like young woman. Precise. Flat shoes and buttoned-up overcoat. And very precise about names. He opened the drawer of his desk and took out a hypodermic syringe and a bottle of colourless fluid. Yes, her manner was almost German. And yet — it was not the manner of old Germany. Correct, but not courteous, the humane being somehow eliminated.

'Very good,' he said. 'You will pay three guineas for each injection. I will give you one now after I have examined you, and one tomorrow.'

'That's very expensive.

'It is what I charge. If it is too much,' he shrugged. 'This is not a charity after all. It is not a matter for your National Health.'

'Can I pay you in any other way?' The girl did not amplify her meaning by tone or gesture.

'In what other way?'

'You are not too old for sex.'

The veins in his temples stood out and his face went purple. 'God in Heaven!' he shouted. 'Have you no shame! I am a doctor not — not some filthy ponce !' He thrust his hands into his pockets, then took them out again. He thought of his wife and family.

This filth, this disease, should not touch his home. He would confine his failure to the times on the brass plate outside. A dim memory of Dr Emmanuel Rat flickered on the edge of his mind like a warning. 'You will pay me money, do you understand? Now take off your clothes.'

The girl stood up and without taking her eyes from the doctor's face, she unbuttoned her coat. Her swollen belly showed all too clearly. She was at least three months pregnant. The doctor had to thrust his hands in his pockets again to keep from striking her.

'Get out!' he spat at her. 'Get out at once.

She took a backward step, as if in fear, and picked up her handbag. The young man who had been waiting in the other room walked into the surgery without knocking.

'Hi, doc. *Wie gehts*?' he said, leaning against the door. Dr Ostbahn passed a weary hand over his eyes. 'Please go away. I can see nobody else tonight.'

'I'm not somebody else, doc. I'm like a riff on the same theme. We're the same abscess.'

'What do you want?'

'I want part of the action, baby.' The young man smiled pleasantly.

'Get out of here!'

The young man took the handbag from the girl. He put his hand inside it. 'Bang bang! You're dead Fritz,' he said.

'Get out of here before I call the police.' The doctor seized the telephone and stood rigid, waiting for them to go.

'Nasty old kraut,' said the young man, and switched on the tape-recorder in the handbag.

'I am a doctor not an abortionist.'

'How much?'

'First I must examine you. We will talk money afterwards.'

'No. First I must know how much you charge, Dr Ostbahn.'

'Very good. You will pay three guineas for each injection —' The young man switched it off and then snapped his fingers.

'Swinging record, eh doc?' He gave the bag back to the girl. 'Split now baby. Take this home and keep it warm. The good doctor and I have business.'

She closed the door quietly behind her and neither of them spoke until the street door clicked shut. Then the young man sat in the swivel chair and swung his feet up onto the desk. He plaited his fingers together over his chest and smiled at Dr Ostbahn.

'Now what seems to be the trouble?' he said.

The doctor stood in the middle of the room, completely lost. It had all happened so quickly. He could not seem to assimilate what had happened, or indeed see quite how it applied to him. His mind was a blank. He waited for righteous wrath to take over and sweep this insolent young lout out of his chair and out of his life. But it didn't come; at least, not in any titanic proportions.

'Will you please remove your muddy feet from my desk,' he said stiffly.

'Not now,' smiled the young man.

The doctor's anger flickered and died. He needed time to think but his mind refused to focus. It skittered away like a tiddly-wink pressed by a big heavy thumb.

'What are you going to do?' he asked.

'Well now...' The young man gazed at the ceiling. 'We could take ten per cent of all the foreskins you collect. You see, I'm going to start a trend towards balaclavas for budgies. A kraut name in that line would be a big leg-up, you know, folks remember. Or then, again we could lance that engrossed bank account of yours.'

'I don't understand.'

'Sit down, dad. Take the weight off.'

The doctor sat heavily in the patients' chair.

'Now what is it you don't understand?'

'What do you want — money?'

'Go on.' The young man leaned forward and rested his chin in his hand, very eager-beaver.

'You — you want money to destroy the recording?'

'Go on.'

'You will give it to the police if I refuse to pay you. You will —' the doctor swallowed hard — 'you will destroy my reputation.'

'Well, I'm sorry, you haven't won the king-sized refrigerator, but you're still in the running for a crack at the one-week-just-reminiscin'-holiday in Israel. Do you want to go on?'

'I want you to tell me what you want from me.'

'Just when you were doing so well. You were bang on the nose about the threat. No flies on you, eh? Course I spotted the cerebrations behind those guesses and put two and two together. They weren't lucky guesses — not on your life. There was real teutonic thoroughness behind them. Method. You eliminated sex.' The young man held up his hand and folded down one finger. 'I probably wouldn't fancy you and anyway Luther was always a stickler for no feeling on a first date. Quite right. Don't let those decadent Rhinelanders tell you different — all that yodelling and leather shorts. It sullies the race. Next. I was just a head case. No, unless Miss Smith was too. Next. I was in it for the bread.' He folded down a third finger and watched it rise again. 'Sharp old dog. You guessed that I was motivated by an index finger.'

'Tell me how much you want, please,' said the doctor, who had barely understood a word. 'I will pay it if I can.'

'I want a piece of the action. You dig?'

'What is the action?'

'There you go again, dad. Look, it's no good trying to con me. I know all about you. You're king of the crochet hook scene baby. And I want to sit in.'

'Will you please talk English. I cannot understand what you are saying.' A fear grew in the doctor's mind. This madman must want narcotics. He recognised some of the vocabulary that he was using. He had seen it in his daughter's magazine, a terrible rag devoted to teenage music. He must be a rock and roll fanatic. He wanted purple hearts.

'You want purple hearts,' he said quickly.

'You know, I wonder about you,' said the young man, shaking his head. 'I think you should loosen your *pickelhaube*. It must be stewing your brains. Where do you get purple hearts from?'

Dr Ostbahn bit his thumbnail. Was the question rhetorical or did he want to know how to obtain them? He gave an equivocal answer.

'I don't know.'

'You're too hot-headed, you know that? Too mercurial by half.'

The doctor just sat staring bleakly at the door. The young man took his feet off the desk and stood up. He stood over the old man and placed his hands on the bowed shoulders. His face was an inch from Otto Ostbahn's.

'Now listen, you stupid squarehead. I'm spelling it out for you. You won't touch anything over a month. I will. Next time a female comes in here and she's fatter than a month, you don't say "*ach Gott*, I'm a doctor not an abortionist". You give her to me, got it? You say, "I haf zis, how you say, colleague — he vill help you".'

Protests welled to the doctor's lips; it was too horrible. He would have to work with this gangster until the police caught them both. And his wife — oh God, what if his wife should find out? The last remnants of his professional pride feebly stirred themselves.

'How do I know that you know what you are doing? How do I know that you won't kill some poor girl?'

'You don't.'

The doctor surfaced for the third time. 'I shall never be able to rest knowing that I have sent some poor young girl to — to —' His mouth quivered with emotion. 'And the risk —'

'I could only kill them. There's a choice of five ways.' Again, he held up his fingers and counted them off as he spoke. 'Septicemia. Peritonitis and a gang of gassy bacilli. Right? The fastest way to go upstairs is by embolism. Zap — good-bye mummy. Then last, you got shock.'

Dr Ostbahn covered his face with his hands, rolls of fat protruding between like a fat man in a wicker chair. His face was sweating.

'And the fuzz. Oh man, the fuzz are hip. Towels, sheets and mattresses under the lights for stains. Obstetrical fluid stains, douche stains, soap stains, blood stains. Breakdown on the drugs in the bedside cabinet. Question the neighbours, question the husband, question the doctor. Fingerprints.' He grinned at the frightened old man.

'I'll tell you something doc. It doesn't scare me one little bit. I take care. I've taken care for eight years. I like what I do and I do it well. I like all of it — all the thrills and spills. I like catching gutless squares like you. See, I know all your tumblers. Old, seedy, running down, hot on excuses. All mouth, no action. You're the kick-start model.'

The young man got up and buttoned his coat. The doctor had begun to cry.

'In a day or so I'll let you know your contact. You needn't put me on the plate outside. I'm your silent partner. Also —' he pointed, very Method, at the baggy old heap on the straight-backed chair — 'don't try telling me that business is slack. I want at least three a week even if you have to drum for work. Even if you have to screw them yourself. And I want Aryans too, you dig? You'll never know that the potbelly in the chair isn't another Miss Smith.'

He flung his arm up in a Nazi salute.

'*Noch einmal* eh, doc? Stay in the bleachers. I'll be hearing from you.' He closed the door quietly behind him.

Part Two

1

God hovering might have seen the hurrying figure on the ground as a circle enclosing a smaller circle; a Mexican asleep in a child's puzzle; a mott and bailey castle on the hoof. Shop windows caught the hurrying figure for an instant amid pyramids of tins, released, lost, and overtaken in an ever-changing context.

Joseph wore his Frank Sinatra hat aslant, a turret; beneath, his cigarette menaced the empty street. Drops of rain pattered suddenly on the resonant straw of his hat. He swore, turned up the collar of his coat and hurried on. In his right-hand pocket he clutched a small bottle containing approx. one teaspoonful of his sperm. He had to keep this warm. On the bottle was a label which read: *The Dose. Keep Away From Children.* It was signed with a skull and crossbones motif.

He turned abruptly into a street of small mean houses. The upper windows streamed by in diagonal perspective each holding, immobile, a grey, oily, square of sky. The rain increased and he ran the last few yards to fling himself at the brass knocker of number 23. Sheltered by the porch the furious din on his hat ceased, and he leaned against the door, immediately stationary, as if all movement were motored by his hat and tumult a symptom of its working. Then he remembered his cigarettes and sprang to life. He removed all but one, secreting the naked remainder in his inside pocket, and returning the packet to the left-hand pocket. He always did this when he visited.

John was out. Turning, grievously offended, Joseph caught sight of the key projecting from under the mat. Clearly, a trusted pal might enter. The hall was in darkness and the light wouldn't come on. He stood fiddling hopelessly with the switch, then he remembered the meter under the stairs and, by matchlight, rammed a grudged shilling piece into the slot.

'Like living in a fucking jukebox,' he said.

The lights came on and the radio in the kitchen, off station, hummed into life. 'It's all happening,' he said. He glared around the empty kitchen. 'Where is that bastard?'

Joseph stood in the centre of the room resting after delivering the three sentences, then emitted a series of little clicks in token of bitterness and disapproval. Next he opened the oven door and placed the small bottle inside, lit the gas, slammed the door and, after much deliberation, turned the dial to Regulo 9. He flung off his wet coat and jacket and bent to tug off his boots. A cascade of rain, hitherto dammed within the confines of his hat, fell from his bent head anointing his socks and his discarded jacket. His ciga-rettes emerged blotched and limp. Swearing, he placed them neatly spaced around the bottle in the oven. The scene in the oven now resembled some occult and anti-Christ ritual, the whole bathed in the unearthly light of the blue, flickering gas-jets.

'Where the hell is that bleeding git? What time does he call this?' Joseph's questions went unanswered. Ever-questing though man's spirit is, Joseph's pursuit of these truths quickly spavined to a halt. He took off his hat and shook the rain from it. He looked at himself in the cabinet mirror. He looked like a slick newborn stoat. Like the fabled unicorn glued to the glass by the singularity of its horn, Joseph was a pushover for a mirror. Much of his leisure was spent trying to increase the impact of his image. His best feature was his teeth. Rows of square white teeth set amid scenic bathos. He pondered. Teeth told in a snarl. He snarled. But snarls were infrequent things; MGM rationed them to a few pre-credit outbursts; Lenin counselled the use of terror seldom, swiftly and all at once. He essayed the boyish grin, dab-bing gauchely at a forelock as gamin and unruly as Hitler's bunker.

He sat on a kitchen chair, thought hard and came up with eat-ing. The same old impasse had been reached. Oh that he could wear his teeth in his hat or perhaps as a crisp white fender under his nose.

The kitchen held nothing of interest. He began to sing to cheer himself up, holding the fork in the attitude of a microphone, and making extravagant movements on the chair.

'I gotta girl, name is Bony Moroni, She's as thin as a sticka macaroni.'

He hadn't thought of that song for years, last heard it fighting it out with the switchback on Blackheath fairground, an oldie but a goodie. Nostalgic.

If John didn't come back soon he'd have to go or the doctor's would be shut. He was worried about the sample in the bottle, about the whole business. He felt aggressive towards the medical profession for requiring such a sample even though they were, as yet, unacquainted with it. It had been his own idea and he suffered lapsed-Catholic pangs about the venal character of the culling. He thought of Onan. Onan had beaten his meat and the Lord had risen up and put the boot in. Blood and seed all over. Fucked confession for another week.

Catholicism had drooped when he came to university, bit the dust as he opened the EUP Marx. He had grown instant proletarian parents toiling against a Lowry backdrop of scurrying antmen and dark satanic mills. There was injustice everywhere. A man could hardly stand up right, let alone sit tall in the saddle in a world where a wank was a sin and the capitalists rode chortling over the peasants' grain.

After a while his thoughts grew confused, an incredible scouse of fag-ends and half-digested concepts, the whole soused with the lemony flavour of bitterness. Twenty minutes passed. Then in came John.

'Hiya, Joseph,' said John brightly, quite pleased to see him. 'What brings you here?'

'You bleeding asked me!' shouted Joseph and got off a snarl. 'What time do you call this?'

'I don't remember asking you to call — not that I'm not pleased to see you.

'Well you did.' He let a huff aristocratise his pale features.

'Okay then, I did.' John was easy.

A hurt whine now crept into Joseph's tone, his usual proposal for wooing. 'I suppose you've forgotten the rest of our conversation last night too.'

John sat down and considered. 'I seem to remember it was about reproduction. You were worried about your dynasty.'

'Yes. Well. I've taken steps.'

'Steps, eh.' Thinking, mucho mystery here.

'I'm getting the doctor to run a check on me. I have to know the Truth. I've got a sample for him.'

John cocked his head, advancing one ear to catch, as it were, every last rung of Joseph's steps. 'Sample?' he offered.

'Sperm.' Joseph took the hurdle with a small blush. 'A sample of my sperm. Well — I've got it, see, and I'm bringing it round.' Very defiant, expecting blockade.

'Bringing it round. How do you mean exactly "bringing it round"? Vinegar on the temples? Flapping at it with a towel? Sounds a pretty dozy sample.'

'Oh Christ, John! Give over dad. Look. Listen, I'm bringing it round to Dr Ostbahn for examination. See? I've got to keep it at body temperature.' His features now registered earnestness because it was his health, and expressed this by a knitting of the brows, a gathering in of the mouth. His hat moved slightly with the contractions.

'Good. Stout fellow. Where is *it*?'

'I put it in the oven.'

'You *what*!'

'I put it in the oven.'

'*In* the oven?'

'Sure — you didn't come and I was afraid it — well Christ man, I had to keep it warm didn't I?'

'He put it in my oven,' John said tonelessly, as one bereaved. 'I cook in that oven. It's a sanitary area. It has gleaming white walls and a door to keep all the goodness *in* and all the nasty dirt *out*! So you come along and stick your sperm in it to warm. Do you do that sort of thing in your own home? No, I bet you don't. Do you think I want your rotten old seed whipping about in my shepherds pie? For your information I don't! You're a dirty bugger.'

Joseph yelled at him. 'It's in a bastard *bottle* you daft sod! It can't get *out*!'

'I suppose you've had a shit in my pillowcase while you were waiting. And put my —'

'I wish l had!'

'— put my toothbrush under your armpit.'

John stamped over to the oven and twisted open the door. He squatted down to see in. A choked cry escaped him and his jaw dropped. Thus: 'Aaaaaargh !' Then: 'No! No! Keep away — *Oh*

God! Horrible, horrible !' He clutched at his throat and fell back onto the carpet.

Joseph erupted from the chair with a great squeak of boots, agog, aghast. 'What is it? What's up?'

A wavering finger pointed into the oven: John seemed to be fighting for words. 'In there — in the baking tin. A little man — homunculus in a hat — gas too high —'

Their cheeks almost touched as Joseph bent to peer into the depths: heat buffeted against his face; his forehead prickled. The little bottle stood in the centre of radiating columns of cigarettes like a little monarch. He burst out laughing.

'Oh come on mate. Pull the other one.' He went back to his chair, annoyed to find it on its back. 'You've blown ya mind. Daft sod.'

'I saw him, I tell you. You don't believe I saw a little man?'

'Get off.'

'Inconceivable, you think?'

'You're darn tootin'. You must think I'm mental or something.'

'You think I'd entertain a figment in my oven?' John passed a weary hand over his face. 'Overwrought — working too hard — irregular diet and that. Bereaved too. But — the mind plays strange tricks, Joseph. Little high-heeled boots stamping on the baking tin. Spectral Zapateo. No, no, you're right. It cannot be; and yet — ? We've only scratched the surface, Joseph, the surface of knowledge, for all our pride. The unknown...'

'Up you.'

'*Das Unbekannt* yawns beyond our ken, God wot.' John shook his head slowly as if returning from a queer reverie. 'Help me into a chair, old fellow. Nasty turn...'

His head bobbed on his neck with each great laboured breath. Joseph stared at him and gnawed his lip. He put his hands in his pockets and then he took them out. He whistled a soundless whistle. He was completely at a loss. It was an act and a bad one too. And Joseph had never — for a second perhaps? — never believed that there was someone in the oven. 'I may be Arts,' he thought, 'and I know about the Twin Cultures and all that crap, but I'm not a bleeding half-wit. What does he take me for? It's insulting. He's twisted. Bent. Definitely. Strictly the surgical boot man.' But he did feel unnerved. He had an awful feeling that John, inert now in the chair, would have given this crazy act whether he, Joseph, had been there or not. After a while he spoke. 'Do you want to come along with us to the quack? We can have a coupla pints after.'

John was lured out of his grand wreck by trivia. '"With *us*"?'

'Oh for chrissake !' He jabbed his preserved cigarette into his mouth and lit it, abrupting smoke at the stupid haperth in the chair.

John made his face apologetic. 'Old man,' he said, 'I don't know how to tell you this — but the sample — it will be dead.'

'That's your fault then!'

'I can't help it. You should have gone straight round there in the first place instead of incinerating it in my oven. Why bring it to me? You want me to be your manager or something?'

'Because I wanted your advice. You're supposed to be my mate. Anyway, I won't ask you now.' Great dignity in the face of betrayal. Switch to pathos: 'I can't just go off and produce just like that. I'm not a bleeding rubber tree you know. And I was a Catholic.'

John made an effort to suppress hilarity. 'Look Joseph, rinse the bottle and get a fresh sample. Take the bottle to the lav.'

'Huh. I couldn't concentrate. It's impossible if I know you know.' He would not be persuaded and would not stop even for a cup of tea. He left the cigarettes too, which more than anything impressed John with the seriousness of the breach.

Joseph applied damp thumb to bell and squirted distant chimes out of the old house. Nobody came. He made the noise of tsk, substance of scratchy mood, nobody kept on not answering tonight, and squirted anew. On either side of him in the porch, laurel bushes dying of dog-piss dripped melodiously. Nothing was distinct in the front garden for the light from the street lamp petered out several doors away, but he could make out a broken hoe, gangs of dandelions, and some sodden newspaper. The brass plate was strictly, he thought, for braille readers. This was one palsied practice and Ostbahn would never pick up his bed and walk.

He furiously rang some more until lights — *TILT* — came on in the hall.

'You've left it a bit late,' said the man. Mid-twenties, white-coated, annoyed, in no special order. Joseph didn't really look at him because he never really looked at greengrocers, fish-fryers, tobacconists, cops or conductors. They were what they did; you read their sign. Anyway, doctors were there to look at you.

He was in the consulting room and seated before the doctor could enter the room, brow ready furrowed with his problem.

'What's up with you then?' asked the doctor, leaning one fist on the desk and yawning at him.

Joseph found his manner very uncongenial. This doctor didn't seem to realise that his role was to be reassuring and sympathetic. Not bleeding rude. Probably saving it up for his private patients. Now Joseph's mother had instilled in him a sense of his rights before the panel, had swung the infant Romulus under the teat for cod liver oil and malt and milk and shots at metronome intervals; he was unlikely to take any wooden nipples tonight.

'I'm worried about personal potency,' he snapped.

The doctor laughed unfeelingly. 'Brewer's droop or the old war wound?' he asked.

'You can cut that out for a start. It ain't funny. What do you do when a mental patient comes in, catch your thumb? I want to know if I can give girls babies or...'

He waved his hands.

'Morally you mean?'

'No, I don't mean morally. Why would I ask your permission? Use your loaf. The priest is for that. I want to know if my stuff is the goods — if I'm capable of reproducing. You can check that on the National Health, can't you? Give a sample to frogs or rabbits or something?' Everybody was a wise guy tonight.

'I'd be glad to do that little thing for you,' said the doctor, 'only we ain't got frogs and we ain't got rabbits. Also we ain't got a microscope. I can give you a note to the hospital if you like?' He sat at the desk, picked a pen from the blotter and wrote the date on Dr Ostbahn's headed notepaper. 'Name?'

'Joseph Clark, no "e". You'd better put c/o University History Department, because I move a lot.'

The doctor wrote away very awkwardly with his left hand for a few minutes and then put the note in an envelope and sealed it. 'I bet you're hell with those campus chicks?' he surprisingly said, squinting at the patient like a horse-player. A cigarette hung from the side of his mouth. Joseph thought he was pretty hip for a doctor.

'Some,' he said, very blasé, modestly exposing the tip of the iceberg.

'I'll bet you do. You do all right.' The doctor was grinning at him, a good guy after all.

'It helps coming from London. Sharp threads and like that The competition is strictly hick up here — you know, fat pants and windsors. Very Dogpatch.'

'Yes, style seems very important to women,' said the doctor.

Joseph saw a caution in the verb and adroitly changed his tack. 'Of course style isn't everything, in fact it's pretty trivial. What is important is — well, naive I guess — is old-time heart. Warmth. Feeling. Sincerity. Like that.'

'Feeling is important in a relationship.' The very faint emphasis was not lost on Joseph and he grinned. They were both men together, having a bit of a larf; they both knew the score. Joseph flashing the pearlies as a treat, said: 'You sure spilled a bibful, babe.'

'Okay,' said the doctor.

'Doesn't hurt, does it?'

'That's right,' said the doctor.

Expansiveness and biography seemed in order. The desk lamp cast a very intimate glow over the homely old furniture and put a bucolic ruddiness into closed city faces.

'You're from the States?' Joseph asked, happy in his flex-roll Oxford with the important extra collar button at the back.

'New York.'

'Man, you're lucky! The Promised Land. That's where I'm going after I graduate. I'm going to drain out my brains to the Village Vanguard, the Five Spot and 52nd Street.'

'It ain't all laughs,' the doctor said after a pause. 'Believe me, some of the kicks are in the groin. You want —' he pointed to Joseph's lapel, 'to leave the buzzer at home.'

'Yeah, I know. They'll probably try and stop me getting in. I'm in the CP too. A plague bacillus.' No harm in letting the brains show a little: the Historian to the Doctor. 'Still, I don't have to tell Them that do I? You gotta use your loaf. Are you going back?'

'Let's just say that I can't.'

'CIA?'

'It wasn't the Comanche.'

This doctor was a character. Joseph memorised the comeback, envied the uptake, deleted the quotes. It was great to be syncopating with an intelligent man after the baffling session at John's house. John was clever but he wasn't a *now* person; the delivery was wrong. He would be square enough to call this repartee.

'A buck on the side doesn't hurt, what do you say?' said the doctor.

'I'm not against it.'

'Take what you can when you can, eh?'

'As long as nobody's hurt.'

This brought a slight check to the fast, flat flow of things and Joseph sensed a squareness in his scruple. He stood up and put his foot on the chair. It seemed to him that this reasserted his style.

The doctor continued. 'It seems to me they've really got the little guy nailed down over here. These — Tories? You can't get near the gravy for antecedents.'

Joseph nodded. 'Did you know that ninety per cent of the wealth is owned by ten per cent of the population and eighty per cent of the land by five per cent?'

'Is that a fact?

'The Press won't print that. We reckon we're doing well to get a mention in the blats. We need a revolution to get those facts in balance.' His face set hard for action and he lifted one of the doctor's Luckies on the strength of their solidarity in the great share-out to come. The doctor lit it for him.

'I had you figured for a pacifist,' he said, indicating the badge again.

'Oh, the badge — yeah, that's for FP. Foreign Policy.'

'Uh-huh. You have strong principles, don't you? Commitment. I like that in a man.'

'How do you get on with the old doctor?' asked Joseph, guessing further ground for empathy.

'Ostbahn is a real asshole. Professional etiquette forbids me to spill my guts about that asshole's activities. Him and his fifty guinea letters.'

'His letters?'

'Oh hell — I don't mind telling you. He works with a psychiatrist on the old abortion thing. For fifty guineas you get a letter saying you're too unstable to have the baby then the brain raper puts his cross on it and you're off to the private nursing home. That's private enterprise, professor.'

'Well, Christ, why don't you report the bastard? That's bleeding criminal!'

'That's a laugh. With my political record? They'd crucify me. Oh no, professor, I tread carefully. I don't go near the fuzz. I'm getting the figures in balance in my own way.' He gave a tight smile and stabbed out his cigarette on Dr Ostbahn's blotter. He seemed greatly preoccupied with dousing random sparks and did not look up. Joseph felt that the relationship was on the edge of slipping away from him.

'How?' he asked.

The young doctor put his hands behind his head and stared over Joseph's head at the plaster oak-cluster on the ceiling.

'Classified, professor.'

The brush-off cut Joseph to the quick. He saw himself suddenly as an outsider, a mouthy student not to be dealt in on the plans of pros. He made his play. 'Look, don't think I'm a stoolie or something. You're worried because it's not legal? What's legal to me? Legal schmegal. Capitalist legal is the big zero, right? Free thinking ain't legal here. Slums are. Poverty is. War is — it's all relative.'

The doctor was clearly impressed. He looked straight at Joseph and saw a man. And that was how Joseph got on the pay-roll of SC Second Chance, proprietor B Herod. The plan was simple. Ostbahn, the psychiatrist, the whole Tory swindle, were to be undercut by a socialist co-operative. Second Chance gave just that to any woman poor or desperate enough to contact him.

The doctor, Ben Herod, spoke rapidly and directly, folding down his fingers as he made a point, tapping the blotter for emphasis. Joseph did the nodding. 'And it's free — absolutely free. We don't even charge expenses. Our group has been allocated a sum by the Party because they see our work as vital. If the state did it we wouldn't need to. There is a constant demand for SC. The danger lies in the hustlers like Ostbahn on one side and the cut-price cracksmen on the other, not in the function. You dig so far?'

'I dig,' Joseph said, hung up completely by the glitter and splash of the principles the doctor was jettisoning in his explanation. Joseph worriedly tried to scurry ahead and sink his own so as to be free and fertile for the new ideas as they were unfolded. It was quite a regatta.

'We need a man on the campus and I think you could be that man. It's not important but you get five pounds for each applicant and if this bugs you you can plough it straight back into

Party funds. You keep your lip buttoned and your ear to the ground and if that strikes you as too gymnastic we can call it off now.' He waited for Joseph's answer.

'When do I start?' said Joseph, like they do in movies.

'You just did.' They shook hands across the desk.

'I'll phone you every day at 6pm to see what you've got. I realise it won't be much until after the Easter freak-out, but see what you can do. Also, another guy will be phoning you every so often with applicants to pass on to me. We thought it would be quite a joke if we got him to call himself Ostbahn and feature this German accent, so just play along.'

Joseph permitted himself a grin. 'Confusing for the fuzz too, if they're listening in.'

'That's right,' said the doctor, 'but if you stay in the bleachers the fuzz won't be listening in, Okay?'

Joseph unleashed his high sign.

2

'Thank you for your trouble,' said John for the third time, following the receiver on its downward path to the cradle. What a waste of fourpence. Straightening, he noticed that his breath had conjured a small grinning Chad from the surface of the mirror:

'The General Public,' he thought, 'the fetid bloody general bloody public. My old man writ large. Only at home in the Public phone box and the Public Lavatory! They left the touch of their breath clinging round the receiver; they left tattered unnameable parcels of filth, foetus and cat's pee in the directory shelf; they drew Chad on the mirror and signed it, like they signed everything else, with a greasy, collective thumb-print. No wonder Caesar passed out.'

John barged out of the booth, his problem unsolved. He needed a dark suit for his father's funeral that very afternoon. He had phoned two outfitters but neither of them seemed able to understand what he meant by Mourning Dress. Obviously they were thick, and probably crooked too: They both wanted £3 a day for the hire.

'£3 a day!' cried John.

'Cleaning and, pressing, sir,' said the outfitter.

'Oh come on.'

'And wear and tear.'

Shrunk lapels after funerals and torn flies after weddings,

John supposed. He stood in the middle of the pavement undecided. Scraps of paper fluttered about his legs: a passing dog looked at him without interest; a member of the general public went into the phone box.

He'd have to borrow a suit from someone. Who did he know well enough to ask? Joseph had suits but Joseph was about a foot high. Most of the University had gone home for the Easter holiday. Except for the Africans, of course. They shivered out a cold Passion in the Law Department Library, and he didn't know any.

'Colin Bell,' he said, snapping his fingers.

Of course Colin Bell—King of Recriminations. He was so tied up in local politics that he could never go home. And he was the right size. And he had a black suit.

John remembered that he had bought the suit on the occasion of the now famous demise of Reg Seeds. The demise had become so famous that John had difficulty in remembering exactly what had happened; what his eyes had seen had been so transformed by the lenses and persiflage of the Press that it had become two events, one on Ellis Street period and one on Ellis Street nerve-centre of a busy, warm-hearted fishing city. Mr Seeds had paused, on his way to work, canteen dishwashing—to buy a flag for Oxfam Day. He put a three-penny piece, distinctly remembered, into the tin and the vendor had pushed a flag into his lapel, pricking his chest and killing him. Mr Seeds, a lifelong haemophiliac and pigeon fancier, had collapsed at once, giving generously in a rush what he had hoarded for fifty years. Colin Bell was there before the civic swabs, getting the facts, poking his huge nose like a microphone into the faces of startled witnesses and generally rolling back the stone. A new, significant Seeds emerged from his articles—*A Local Schweitzer*; the faithless were vilified—*Townhall Silent on Seeds* and *Papal Indifference*? The flag vendor, an elderly widow, fled abroad in fear of a murder rap. The noise lasted a week and was interred with the remains of Mr Seeds, for which Colin Bell bought the suit and at which he circulated a petition.

John set off for City Square to find him.

'Hello there,' shouted Colin Bell, jigging his banner up and down at the head of a crocodile of marchers. 'Looking for me? Grapple on.'

John fell into step beside him. It was just the day for a march, with a strong inspiriting wind in the air. To his left a guitarist in a forage cap strummed a plangent beef and all around him the banners flapped and slapped. John wondered what they were marching about for the banners offered a broad menu for redress.

'I wanted to see you about my father's funeral,' John said.

'Sorry about that. Dreadful business. I meant to call round but I've been up to my eyes in it.' Colin's banner wavered dangerously as he clapped at John's shoulder the clap of condolence.

The procession came to a ragged halt at the traffic lights and most of the bearers rested their banners on the ground.

'Bloody heavy these things,' said Colin, massaging his arms, and wiping a mucal caste mark onto his forehead with his handkerchief.

'You want one of those metal cups. You know, you wear it on a strap just over the navel.

Colin turned eagerly — 'Can you get hold of them?'

'You could try the scout shops.'

'No, that's out of the question, of course,' said Colin. 'We have imposed sanctions against the scouts.'

The marchers set off again flanked by cars and women with shopping bags who paused to watch them. A policeman looked at them and then set his watch. John remembered the feeling of being looked at. He had marched down this street ten years ago, an aching profile in the Boys' Brigade, and five years before that a blushing Cub. He looked at Colin marching. Bags of swank, narrow chest thrown out, hips shuddering like panniers on a mule. Around his mouth and chin sprang short, reddish hairs, a beard like a distraught magnetic field that exactly caught his public image. On some fairy morn the wind had changed and petrified for ever these bristles of his expostulation.

'Colin?' said John at last. The huge nose swung round to him.

'Colin? It's about that black suit. Could I borrow it for my father's funeral?'

'I don't see why not, old chap. When is the funeral?'

'This afternoon.'

'Well. You could have it for a couple of hours or so, but I must have it back by six.'

'Yes that's okay,' said John.

Cohn narrowed his eyes down from mere slits to blackheads and contemplated John.

'We could do a deal on this,' he said. 'You probably saw the news this morning. Twenty-two Vietcong shot down in cold blood. We're having a demonstration tonight — a march on the town hall. People just read about an atrocity like that and then turn to the racing results. That's why we're marching! Somebody's got to step in and stop it!'

A fine spray played over John throughout this discourse and he nodded repeatedly to avoid saturation of any one spot.

'Where do you stand?' sprayed Colin.

'I think someone should step in and stop it,' said John.

'Six o'clock, Queen's Park then. I've got a job for you. Oh yes — and wear the suit. I don't know how you can bear to be seen in that Fascist outfit. Something has got to be done about this Vietnam thing. People have got to be made to sit up. It's the numbing bloody apathy that's so shocking. So long as they've got their tellies and tigers in their bloody tanks they're as contented as castrated cats!' He continued in the same varicose vein for two intersections, dampening where he sought to inflame.

'Sit up and step in and stop it,' thought John, caught on the rhythmic hook. He wished he were somewhere else. He wished he could suddenly drop a big mirror in front of Colin Bell and watch an embarrassed red crawl over the yakking features, watch him fall onto his knees and plead for a lobotomy. They had never liked each other, had not in fact spoken since Colin had tried to veto the projected von Stroheim season as decadent and non-utilitarian. Of the many things that John hated about Colin one thing was uppermost: Colin had the comradely habit of repeating your last word with a nod, and then splashing into vociferous opposition, made all the more splenetic by his momentary lapse. John wondered how a habit like that got started. 'Hell's Bell,' he thought, after Sartre.

'You know they've chucked me out of the LP? Oh yes, the SOBs. The bloody broadcloth bastards! They called me a red for opposing the US in Vietnam. Of course I was able to prove that dissent was a cardinal tenet of socialism and an inalienable human right. And of course the CP threw me out years ago over Hungary so that was eyewash. Eyewash!'

'Ho, ho, ho!' John entered the general merriment, but didn't slap his thighs. 'When can I pick up the suit then?'

'You want it now do you?'

'Well, I do really,' said John, loathing the apology in his tone.

3

Carol felt completely hung up. John had shaken her faith in humanity. She had always believed that everyone regardless of race or intelligence, reflected upon the great eternal triptych — Who are we? Why are we here? Where are we going? She in fact had the Gauguin painting of the same name over her bed, a return to the tonic (non-fizzy) after the secular improvisations of the day. Not everyone admitted their common humanity in public, she knew that. Marxists wouldn't speak personally and Zen Buddhists were hard to pin down, but they all surely knew that they walked the earth alone, and that they would return one day to dust. Now it seemed that there were those who never thought her questions. They ate, slept, made love and died but their motivation, soul and spirit were so alien that they formed a separate species. They were not conditioned into mutation: they were born so. John was one of these.

Carol threw on her tweed coat and covered her hair with a scarf. She never wore gloves. She put her notebook and pencil in her pocket in case of a pensée which was likely as she was going to the park. She always turned to the country for a spiritual fix, for a cosmic echo of her mood. The municipal park was not red in tooth and claw or unmarked by ruinous man, but it was the nearest bit of green.

The park was deserted and as she walked she felt a familiar peace. Hominids and mutants were leashed and no longer fouled the footpaths of her mind. The trees were still black and bare and uncomplicated. Everything was in its ordained place. The air was cold and clear and she filled her lungs with it and clenched her fists in her pockets. She walked around the perimeter of the park and then sat down on a bench. Across from where she was sitting a peacock suddenly materialised and glided over the fence, his tail, shabby now, was still a bright tremor on her retina.

She stared at the watery lemon sun and it seemed to her that it was pierced again and again by the sharp brittle branches until gobs of yellow fell upon the earth. This reminded her of Christ's blood on the robin's breast and she was off, scribbling it all down in her notebook. After a while she found it too cold sitting and so she set off for a final lap. Her feet rang on the earth, an iron collage, she noted, of stamped leaves and rimed mud. On the fence was a lost red glove waving for help; Carol ignored it; human flotsam was so artificial.

All this alchemy was arrested by a strange sight at the end of the rose walk. It was Joseph disporting himself like an ape. He must have seen her before she saw him because he was well into the part. His breath made fat cumulus clouds as he scuttled at random among the empty flower beds, scratching at his armpits, rounding out his jaw into apish curve with his tongue and shattering the silence with feral cries. Carol watched with interest. She didn't laugh until his Cuban heels caught in a root and he crashed, still flensing at his armpits, into a skeletal rosebush. She helped to dust him off, a maternal end to his primal display of plumage.

'Are you all right?' He wouldn't look at her giggling face.

'I fell into that bloody thorn bush.' Joseph snarled back at the gnarled snarl. 'The parkie wants to root that bugger up. What's it in aid of anyway, I want to know. Nasty lump of firewood.'

'Do you want to sit down, Joseph?' asked Carol.

He did, and spreading a *Melody Maker* on the bench, sat.

'I'm sure I've cut my leg to the bone,' he said, working his trouser leg up to expose his stout white leg. 'Christ! Look at that!'

Carol squatted down and saw, through the goatish hair, an almost subliminal incision.

'Those thorns are poisonous you know,' he said, a little nettled by her equanimity. 'It's bound to go septic. Have you ever seen a tetanus case? Just your bloody heels and your bloody head touch the deck.'

'That would put the cinema off your list,' said Carol grinning at him but he was preoccupied. He cupped the dot with shaking hand and fished for a handkerchief.

'No, that's dirty,' said Carol and undid her scarf. 'Here, let me.'

'Is there a first aid post in this park?' asked Joseph enthroned while maiden knelt and tied a silken favour about his calf. She shook her head and tied a bow for a finalist Persian. 'You mean there's nothing?' He was incredulous. 'What is this — the Yukon? If you conked out in here you'd sodding die!'

He looked down on her sleek head bent over his wound. Oh God, why wasn't she his bird? Because he was short and ordinary? No, no — not that. Because his mate John had found her first. And John wouldn't lay her; he had to be crazy. It was wintry in the park but in Joseph's trousers it was perennially spring. Christ, if he didn't get it soon he'd need a wheelbarrow for his bollocks.

'I'll buy you a cuppa tea,' he said and got up. They walked over the frozen mud, Joseph leaning heavily on her arm, to the kiosk at the West Gate.

'Two splosh, luv.' Joseph clicked a florin on the counter. They sat on wrought-iron chairs at a wrought-iron table in the open.

'Don't you want your lumps, Carol?' He liked to use her name because it was good tactics. If she was dancing he was asking; if she wasn't he'd just take another turn around the animals. He had to find out if her affair with John was still current, of course. Meanwhile, there was no harm in laying down some grainy close ups. Their fingers brushed as he took her sugar lumps.

'Two treys,' he said shaking the lumps in cupped hands and then rattling them along the table. 'Bam! Tonight I gotta golden arm!'

'Now throw a single one,' said Carol.

'You saw the film,' cried Joseph, incredulous.

'John made me.'

'*Made you see it*,' he corrected. 'Great movie. You dug it?'

'No. I thought it was boring and gimmicky.'

'Yes — some of it was um —' Joseph drummed his fingers on the table —' trivial.'

Conversation lapsed. Carol drank her tea. She drank it in a series of little sips, moving the cup away from her mouth as she swallowed and then back again, never replacing it in the saucer. Joseph studied her over the rim of his steaming cup. He thought she looked like a slide trombonist on a ballad. Everything about this chick was a ballad. The white in her eyes was faintly blue like Christmas card snow.

'How's the work going?' he asked.

'So-so. I spend too much time on the poetry. I haven't looked at Anglo-Saxon.'

'I know what you mean. Those thegns are extra nothing. Me, I'm all the time at Marx you know. We do a paper on Roman Britain. Dragsvilla.'

Carol smiled and took another sip of tea. Somewhere nearby, a rodenty bunch of birds began chirruping, poetry to some but to Joseph bedsprings. Even a scrap of paper clicking over the frozen dirt did things to his sensitive skin. He couldn't stop thinking about getting his leg over.

'I was surprised to see you here,' she said after a while.

'In the park?'

'Uh huh. I don't know why. I just never pictured you in a park.' Joseph leaned his elbows on the table and his chin on his fists, a pyramid of great charm with a list to the lovely lodestar.

'Just where did you picture me, Carol?' he said.

'Oh, in the city — streets, cafés — you know.' She looked away from him at the line of gaunt trees. She turned up the collar of her coat and then turned it down. She was embarrassed. 'You've always seemed a very city sort of person.'

'People usually think I'm some sort of yob out of his nut with noise and kicks and —'

'No, I don't think that Joseph.'

Joseph. She'd used his name at last. He had scored, got through the ladylike pose and hit the button. She was on the run now and anything could happen. The elastic might break, please God.

'People used to talk through me all the time until I got to college. Then they had to rethink see. Hoorah for Joseph the educated ape, you know?' He had an ear like a seismograph for class; deep down in Carol Scott he heard the tiny rustle of a serviette unfolding — battle hymn of the drawing rooms. He could play on the inherited guilt of the bourgeoisie, earned by the Wobblies, the Communards, the Catalans, and played now on a hipster's barrel-organ.

'You know, Carol, people thought I was the Leap in the Dark.'

'Well, you know I'm not like —'

'No, no. I don't mean you, Carol. People,' he nodded, re-membering, 'just people.' He timed it perfectly, the pause, the hands gathering speed and pushing at air to make way for words. 'I have feelings. Not city boy feelings — just feelings, Carol. Period. I don't have many friends but they know me, they know what I care about. For one thing, I dig the country. So it's corny. I dig —' he closed his eyes and tried to recall what was in the country, some corn for this free-range chick. He had last seen it at fifteen, a mistake, and had stood in a field staring at a cow for ten seconds before making —'Okay, I seen that. Now where's the action?'— for the railway. All that kept coming to him was the refrain, 'Beans could get no keener reception in a beanery.'

'I dig,' he said, 'mountains and greenery, beans —' Oh Christ, that slipped out. What had she said to Jane that time? At that no-mark party? 'Trees, cows, sticks and all like that.' As Joseph opened his eyes it came to him.

'I sometimes think that its only in the country you can really find your own rhythm. It's like a personal thing you know, Carol. I can't externalise it worth a damn.' He waved a wrist in self dismissal.

'I know what you mean, Joseph.' Carol was smiling at him.

'You know,' he flashed his teeth at her, 'I believe you do.'

'Joseph?' said Carol before he could follow up the teeth with the glims in one of his slow-burn features.

'Yes, Carol.'

'How would you feel if your father died?'

Joseph winced. He thought he was doing better than that. A cup of splosh and twenty minutes on him and Pan had bought him bugger all. John's old man! He said his piece though. What Is A Dad. As he spoke, a clutch of stay-out sparrows galloped home to make it all up with Poppa while he was still alive.

Carol nodded. 'John doesn't give a damn.' Her eyes filled with tears. Joseph's hand sped out to cover hers, his ID made a clang nothing like a brandy barrel on the wrought-iron table.

'No no no you don't believe that Carol. You know he cares about it.'

Carol was crying now. 'He joked about it — the same day.'

Joseph squirted solicitously at her hand. Resuscitation; next move, kiss of life, then perhaps his sticky solution for her knotty problem. But he knew this was the end of the line for him: termi-nus. Joseph would never steal a mate's bird, and John was still his mate. He sprang back from the mental clinch, arms high to show no foul intended.

'He's a very warm guy, Carol, I can tell you that. Personally I rate John one hundred per cent. He's like me—he doesn't flash his feelings around, you dig, but all the time he really cares a helluva lot. It's all locked up inside him. For instance take last night. I took him out and got him drunk and then, boy, the dam really burst…'

'John cried?' Carol stared at him hard, starting a psychogalvanic response in his palms.

'Pretty near. He was really broken up about it.'

'What did he say then?'

'Or you know — how life wasn't worth living and so on.'

'What about his father?'

'Well I guess I'm to blame there. I tried to keep him off that. I figured that he oughtn't to dwell on that — too close to him, you dig.' Joseph was really sweating on this one; what he said could be checked. He tried pushing it over to Carol, keeping his face worried and boyish. 'Do you think I fouled up there, Carol? Is it better to make people face it or —'

'I don't know.'

He ground his fag out savagely. Okay, so he'd been trespassing, but this was getting to be The Biggest Rosary Ever Told.

'You want to hold onto him, Carol — you're good for him. You're a swell girl Carol,' he patted her hand, the Trappist's last feel, 'if you ever need a friend you know you can count on me.

'Thank you, Joseph.'

'I mean it. One hundred per cent. Just call me.'

'Thank you.'

'Day or night.' He drove it all home with his candid gaze, and then brought the bouquet out from behind his back. 'Oh yes, if you're writing in your book there, put this in. Those dried leaves and that frost could be Smith's Crisps with salt. You dig, it's a metaphor.'

'So it is,' said Carol, very surprised. 'Thank you, Joseph.'

'That's okay.' He got up, made a high sign — 'I'm gone' — and limped bravely towards the tall timbers.

Carol watched him until he was out of sight and then yawned enormously. A raffish dog made a three point landing on the crazy paving, dropped a stonehenge of turds, gave two little crouch steps to finish and then bounded off without a backward glance. She didn't put this down either.

4

———————————————

They were all sitting round on their macs on a grassy bit of the park waiting for the funeral march to begin. John, sitting in the coffin, watched them with an uncommitted eye. Colin Bell was everywhere, now checking the banners, now conferring with a bespectacled girl holding a clipper board, waving his arms and shrilling down a gym mistress's whistle that swung from his neck on a crimson sash. As he swept past the coffin, a firebrand in the gathering darkness, John was struck by the multitude of badges on his lapels. One in particular struck him. God is alive and well in Argentina. What could it mean? Musing thus, he now glimpsed Arthur somewhere in the middle distance doing difficult things to an oak tree, a crowd of admiring youths around him. Had Arthur seen the badge? Would a miracle-working goat lead them to the City Square amid the clangour of cymbals and the pibroch of prick-music?

A familiar voice sounded in his ear. It was Joseph, looking embarrassed either for dropping him after the Affair of the Oven or for being seen in this particular context.

'Cock-up innit?' he said, sneering at the assembly.

'Bell seems to know what he's doing.'

'Huh. Him?' retorted Joseph without cockcrow cue. 'He's roped you in at last then. What happened — get turned on?'

'Just a business deal. I borrowed his suit.'

They were a little formal with each other, gingerly putting

weight on the fracture to test it. Joseph squatted on his heels beside the coffin and gazed over to the trees while John whistled a little tune. Both attitudes were meant to convey that they were ready to be nobody's fool at the drop of a hat.

Joseph too had an extra badge tonight. Its message was terse and hand-printed and it glowed with a coating of luminous paint. It said: *Clark*.

'Clark,' read John.

'Eh?' Joseph dangerously narrowed his eyes as he looked at him.

'Your name,' he pointed.

'I thought it would facilitate recognition. I don't wanna get lost in all this crowd.'

This struck John as a bit heretical but he diplomatically said nothing. There was another awkward silence and they both entrenched themselves in the observation of people. In the bushes stood the forbidding presence of the parkie, in his fist glinted an instrument for pinking litter. He licked his lips and waited, hoping.

'What do you think about abortion, John?'

Joseph was biting his thumb, a sure sign, not of worry, but of showing John that he was worried. And with the problem would come the frat pin; a package deal. Exit duo hoofing and waving boaters in unison. Them Two Funky Jays, back in the old I said back in the old routine.

'I think,' said John folding his hands across his chest very Elder Zossima in his box, 'it's very good.'

'What does that mean?'

'Well what do you mean, what do I think?'

'What do you think? Swiss clinics for the rich. The old fifty guinea letter. Cut-price backstreet cracksmen. The moral issue for chrissake. You must have read the papers man.'

'It's an old folk craft like thatching. I'd hate to see it go. There's too much uniformity. Haven't we room for a little insanitary fatality once in a while? Jenkins says we have. What do you say?'

'Crap.'

'Okay. I think they're the last heroes of the century, even the last possible heroes — I haven't worked that out though. I see them as essentially romantic in the sense that knights are romantic, tilting at the biggest dragon in the world with their bright lancets. Not an evil dragon because evil is a greater chimera than dragons. Overpopulation see. So they wipe the slate clean for thousands of unlucky fuckers.'

'A second chance,' Joseph offered.

'Exactly. And yet they're reviled, abused and hunted down by society. The last of the fast guns brought in from outa town to reduce the township of its troublemakers. They bring colour and drama into humdrum suburban lives — a whiff of cordite and mystery.'

'You don't think it's immoral then?' Joseph pursued.

John stared at him in amazement, pitching in lots of jaw-drop and orb-pop before he noticed that Joseph really was worried. He had stopped biting his thumb.

'You must be joking. Without God, that is, until He gets back from Argentina, morality means social expediency. When we're up to 500 million in England the cabinet will have to restore National Service. A new quiet deadly army of cap-fitters, queers, abortionists and interrupter instructors will spring up. Then it will stop being romantic.'

'That's sci-fi baby,' said Joseph doubtfully.

'The truth only.'

On the green the marchers were beginning to form up in ranks, Colin Bell on a tree-stump steed, palm upraised, badges glinting like chain-mail.

'Who have you put up the spout then?'

Joseph was offended. He stood up and brushed at his knees and then checked that his levis hadn't got wedged in the back of his boots. 'I was talking about a social problem.'

'Oh I see,' said John, fed up with this on and off lark. What was up with the silly bugger — painters coming or what?

'It came up at Bell's meeting, that's all. I told them what I thought, pretty well your viewpoint actually, and they came on all square with me.'

'Didn't see it as an essential plank in the hustings next week?'

'It was just a discussion. No policy decision involved,' said Joseph very withdrawn now, eyebrows up in his hat with disdain as he gave John plenty of the old profile.

'Not much drawing power?'

'I'd better split. I don't want to get lumbered with carrying you and that bleeding great box down the road. See you around, dad.'

'There's ants and there's thinkers, eh baby?' John called after him, but Joseph ignored these darts and strode off. Why did he do it, trample his friends' illusions to mash? Was it jealousy or was it his way of showing the leper's-bell round his neck? John decided it signified nothing. It was a meaningless improvisation like all the rest; wig-bubbles and colander farts.

Lying in the coffin, a cassock under his head, John stared at the moving rectangle of sky. The stars were out now but he lacked the ability to identify the Great Bear or the Southern Cross. He guessed that he was drifting down the middle of some wide avenue because no buildings broke on the horizontals of his craft. The jostling was regular and rhythmic. At times lights shone on his outstretched legs, and then again he was moving through darkness. Below, he was fitfully conscious of voices and heavy breathing humming through the wood like a sleeper's saw. His body fell away from him, and his mind, awash between sleeping and waking, recreated fragments of the day.

He saw bright white rows of tombs, yew trees, stone doors without knockers, black solitary people with watering cans, his father's grave at silly mid-off in the clipped green field.

'Okay up there, Democracy?'

John started at the rap of knuckles on wood. Colin Bell's voice.

'Are you all right?'

'Yes, thanks,' he said.

'Not far now.'

John rubbed his eyes, scratched his belly and slowly raised himself on one elbow to see over the side. Stewart Street. Not far, the man sez. About two bloody miles is all. He could see shoulders and bent heads below him, and below that rows of boots; behind him was a forest of banners and beyond that darkness.

Someone saw him and pointed. 'Oi look! The ghost walks!'

'Shut up!' shouted Colin Bell. 'You in the box, lie down!' John lay down and held up a wrist to see his watch, luminous numbers among stars. What a bastard Bell was. Fancy playing a trick like that. He felt his skin hot with embarrassment.

He had worn the suit to the funeral. Carol had been there and Mr Reed from the morgue, the vicar and the sexton. Thank God for small attendances. They had all stared at him. He felt as if he had just been caught pasting a note, three pints please, on the door of a family vault. He had just stood there blushing, gathering handfuls of slack suit into his pocketed fists. 'I know it's a bad fit—' he had said, but Carol dropped her flowers onto the wet earth and ran, her hand clenched to her mouth. How could he have known about the suit? He had worried about the flapping trousers, the tiny shoulders, the hugely wading seat that hung vacantly from his hips; he had not seen the foot high letters on the back of the jacket:

The Corpse of Democracy. Vietnam 1967.

Mr Reed had lent him his mac but nobody seemed to believe him. Well, now it was all over, dust to dust, a dusting off of hands. His father was dead and buried; a useless life, a useless death, a farcical burying. There was a certain consistency in that. Of the blood, only he, John Jenkins, unaligned and uncaring, had attended his funeral, solely in his capacity as an object.

A banner slanted sail-like past the side of his coffin. *Stop This Useless ...* he couldn't see the rest. Roofs hove into view tilted at an angle, telegraph wires and lights and tree tops. They were nearing the centre of town. A voice began singing *We shall overcome* only to be instantly overcome by Colin Bell. 'Shut up you fool! This is a funeral march. Negro rights tomorrow.'

And Uncle Bert? Why hadn't he attended his brother's funeral? Uncle Bert, impresario of the packaged deal box, had been banging at the door, synchronising watches, ordering wreaths and jotting down the time and place of the burial before Mr Reed had finished his embroidery. Then the silly old fool hadn't turned up. Silly old sod. And then it came to John, the, penny clattering down the chute. He had told him two o'clock Monday, even watched him lick his pencil and write it into his battered diary without noticing the twenty-four hour discrepancy. Some earlier funeral had gained Uncle Bert, his glass eye, his open-shouldered acceptance of responsibility, his hair trigger responses from the nave. John wondered when he had discovered his error. He saw Uncle Bert's confident back on the chief mourner's bench, ramrod straight among the ducking and bending of whisperers, the unknown kinsman with one weeping eye. Had he made it through to the ham supper on the crest of their reticence, Uncle Fitzherbert, the blot on the escutcheon? Well, that was Uncle Bert off the Christmas list. He would have to reorientate to a life without Brylcreem and the *Boys' Book of Sport*.

'Keep well to the left. Let the traffic through!' shouted Colin Bell.

Bright faces gazed down at John in his coffin from the top of a bus, their mouths opening and shutting soundlessly like fish. John shut his eyes. Behind his lids he could see Mr Reed's mouth opening and shutting. A lot of it around. They were leaving the cemetery and Mr Reed was telling him something, something that seemed important but he couldn't focus on it because Carol was running again and again and everybody was staring at him. He picked a leaf from the hedge and dug little crescent scars in it with his thumbnail. Was it about his father? John reached back for the words, hearing the voice, the sound of their shoes on the flagstones. He furrowed his brow and squeezed his eyes shut to expel the splinter but nothing came. The coffin lurched suddenly from side to side losing height, and John grabbed at the sides in panic.

'Gently lads! Put it on the steps.'

They laid the coffin gently on the steps of the townhall and then retired to sit cross-legged on the pavement below. Those with hats doffed them. John stared up into the oratorically distended nostrils of the beloved leader. He saw the tiny chest fill with air like an elf's smalls, the bristles gather into some sort of order and then, in a roar, fall back in disarray.

'Comrades!' he bawled. 'We come here not to praise democracy but to bury it !' He waited instinctively for the sturdy throats and honest hands to fall silent again, which wasn't long. 'You all know why we're here tonight. To do honour to a brave concept that first flowered so many aeons ago at the knee of wise Plato the Greek. Yes, Friends. The Greeks were a race of Burkes.'

'Oh Gawd,' said John, prone under the fount of inspiration.

'Don't show your ignorance,' hissed Colin, 'lie still!'

Dere Colin Bell, i hope you are well. Most of us umans are esentialy figurs of fun and our postures ridiculus in the extrem especialy when we are ardent about things. You are the most ridiculus that has ever been seen on earth (by me). You do fulfil a roll but not the wun you think. You are supposed to be angry and cross and mone a lot. Yore words dont matter a fig or tittle jus so long as you keep them up. The Underdog is ment to be a massokisst like a lady is. If you reely wanted to be efective you wood do wot Oswald did exept that is a Rite Wing Thing. The Left wing Thing is to do it to yorseff. Poor petrol on yore self and strik a lite. Do this in the Stranglers Galery in Parlt. It wont do any good but at least you wont look ridiculus. A welwisher.

Colin Bell surveyed his audience. There were few students, so he switched into a lower gear. 'Today we see the death of democracy. Not a quiet death, friends. Not a natural death like you and me expect when our time comes. Not a quick death.'

He pushed his voice up an octave, adjusting the spray to nee-dle-fine. 'It's being murdered! Bombed, riddled and gassed in Vietnam today and everyday!' He flung his arms up into the cru-cified position, held it, then let them fall limply down. 'A little country far away, you say? What has that got to do with us? We're doing nobody any harm — just minding our own business.'

Two policemen pushed through the sitting crowd and came up the steps to the speaker.

'Go home and mind your own business then,' said one of the policemen, quite off the cuff. The police had developed a special method for dealing with Colin Bell. They didn't want to pinch him because his feet smelled from all the marching and, worse, he was a Fabian Farter. (Fabian Farters let their wind run free in any company to establish common clay antecedents.) The smell of C Bell made the cells hard on everybody and led to short tem-pers and rank-pulling on night-shift.

'That was a rhetorical question, officer. Not a statement of my beliefs.' Colin Bell drew himself up to his full height repeatedly. The crowd applauded. It was always the same.

The police and the leader exchanged broadsides of wit and ridicule; if Colin lost he stormed off in a huff; if Colin won the police pinched him and lost.

'You know you're disturbing the peace,' said the less witty policeman.

'Peace!' said Colin. 'Peace!' he screamed. 'What peace? The peace of the deaf dumb and blind? The peace of the rabbit war-ren?'

'Peace off,' said the witty policeman, grinning.

The audience applauded. The less witty policeman leaned over to his colleague and said out of the corner of his mouth:

'Watch the language, George.'

'What peace can there be for us when our brothers are —'

'Hello. What have you got in here?' The witty policeman shone his torch into the coffin. John squirmed in the light of those laughing eyes.'

'While our brothers are —'

'Hop out. Come on, look sharp.'

John clambered awkwardly from the coffin and stood beside it, very diffident in his radical rocker-suit. Fuzz frightened him. The glare of the torch hurt his eyes and made him think of footlights and turns, a thought clearly paramount in the policeman's mind.

'Your brothers are dying. As long as I am permitted to speak I shall continue to —' Colin Bell came to a halt. Horribly, no-one was stopping him. No-one was listening either.

'And what's your name, son?' said the witty policeman, upstaging any possible reply with Method twirdles of his torch.

'I am leather apron,' cried John notwithstanding, and turning, ran away amid great applause.

5

Joseph had a cold. He breathed heavily through his mouth and at intervals sniffed a dragging schlurppy sound like a soundtrack of the monster's end. He too felt as if he were drowning; it was all around him, all inside him and he could barely think for it. After a few hours he had learned to live with it, and looked forward to the good times like when one nostril broke free with a little pop and air rushed in, cold and clear as a peppermint. Somewhere in the centre of all this mucus was the real essential Joseph, damp but rational.

It was this Joseph, blundering about the room and honking into tissue paper who thought now, with the mulled radiance of a peat fire, of love. One day he would meet her, the one for him. Across the crowded room she would see him, love him, touch his hair as she passed his chair, notice his teeth. And the line would be secure: a quiverful of fletched and formidable Josephs to man the barricades. No fool, he saw that Spring would be a little late this year. And the next. Joseph had cased the scene and found only a dearth of Catholic, Marxist, hard-bopping chicks. The schismatic, the bourgeois, the cloth-eared in dull hegemony as far as the beshaded eye could see. But he could wait. He had one hundred per cent, straight up, no shit, litmus-tested proof of his potency from the hospital. Now he knew. He thought of yesterday's events, the mysterious doctor, the humiliation at John's, the loss of his rain-sodden cigarettes. He trumpeted into a tissue and tried to suppress the lot.

The girl from next door thundered on his door.

'Wod id id now?' he shouted. 'Noise of Kleenex hiddig the floor too loud for you?'

'Phone,' she replied, curtly. 'And you'd have heard it if you hadn't ruined your ears.' She stood blocking the way, her hair piled up in curlers under a chiffon scarf.

'Balls,' said Joseph, elbowing past.

'Suck 'em,' the girl replied.

'Ib I had a mouth ad big ad yourd I could.'

'Keep sucking,' she said.

No response had ever been devised in this fugue of flighting, so Joseph lost. He blamed it on his rundown health and turning his back, picked up the receiver.

'Cidy desg,' he said urbanely.

'What? Is that Joseph Narodniki?' Thick German accent.

'No. Joseph Clarg no E. Id thad Ostbhad?'

'Yes, Ostbahn here — Is Herod there then?'

'Dough. Id alride. I cad tage a bessage.'

'But you're not Joseph Narodniki?'

'Alride—I cad be—I ab. I ged id, id alride. Joseph Narodnigi.'

'You are he?'

'Yeb. Shood bub.'

He took down the address and the appointment time and rang off. It didn't seem such a good idea now, this Second Chance, and he wished he hadn't joined. It was only in bed that night that he remembered all the questions he should have asked, would have asked if it hadn't seemed to impugn his uptake. For example, why should the CP care about abortion? It wasn't in Marx. That didn't prove it was all cock of course. It could be in Lenin. Part of the NEP perhaps? That morning at the hospital, sniffing miserably and ejecting seed into a test tube, he had remembered the Kulaks. It was probably to do with them. 'Constrain the Kulaks.' That rang a bell. They voted with their feet, or was that someone else? Joseph kept the problem of the Kulaks and abortion suspended in his mind, uncorrelated but distinctly promising, for a later think-in.

The kettle broke into a whistle as he re-entered his room, and began to boil. He poured it into a bowl and mixed in the Friars Balsam, then burnoused in a municipal slipper-bath towel, he dangled his strangling features over the fumes. Moisture gathered on his skin and hung in minute droplets from his brows. A score of blackheads put forth their heads as both nostrils popped in vernal awakening. Joseph staggered back gasping. 'Man! That's nose candy like mother used to bake!' he thought, rubbing at his face with the limp towel, and returned for another fix which set the fumes coursing along his orifices. A ball of phlegm teetered at the back of his throat and with a giant hawk he sent it winging, fat plop, into the bowl. Joseph couldn't bear to look at it. He reeled to the cupboard and downed six Beechams, poking his tongue around the white residue in the glass. He was determined to beat this cold and he followed every rule like a West Pointer.

He settled back in the armchair and closed his eyes, exhausted for the moment by his own ministrations. He sat still for so long that he became afraid he would fall asleep. Asleep, he knew his mouth would gape, and worse, he would breathe through his mouth and awaken with a throat like a vulture's crutch. An effort of concentration was called for.

He dwelt on his newly established potency. Primitives may delve ditches and impale them with staffs, munch balls of their enemies and tap Calpurnia up in a fast passing; he, Joseph, needed no aids, no crutch for his crutch. Rattling poppy-like with seed, he arose to get the tissues, blew his nose and sat. Yes, he was dangerous to women; a man to be handled with care in the clinches, a left kicker with the aim of a Matthews.

A vast heat descended upon his skin like a sunburn. His eyes prickled. The mucus and the Beechams combined in an enveloping tumescence. Fears and inhibitions melted before his gathering lust. He could have flung himself on the cat or its whiskered cushion but he had neither. Joseph knew, brains descended, that he must have a woman this night or bust.

He flung on pullovers, jumpers, coats and scarves with antic, archive movie haste while his mind sped to a swifter removal. 'I'm rimshot tonight, baby,' he thought, as he lanced through the door, bookgrant crackling in his pocket. On the first landing a door opened to reveal an aged eye and the floral spout of a lavatory-bound teapot. He said hello and the door shut immediately, perhaps forever.

In the telephone box, red the colour of sex, he dialled the number and panted at his image in the mirror.

'Good evening,' said the black plastic receiver.

'Good evedig,' he replied in a pomaded voice.

'Can I help you?'

'I saw the Adverd. Dext to Strig Guverdess.' He had trans-
ferred this phone number from fag packet to fag packet for
months.

'I'm sorry, our regular governess is on her sabbatical but we
can probably...'

'Dough, dough. You dode udderstad. I dode wad the
guverdess.'

'Did you have one of our interviewers in mind, then?'

Joseph felt as if he was shouting underwater. He shouted
louder. 'I dode wad a blarded idderview. I wad a fuggig fug you
twerb!'

'Sorry. I can't seem to understand you. Are you foreign —
coloured?'

Joseph fumed. Discrimination! Chiffon-clad but hideous.
Twice he had banned South African fruit. He prepared to terminate negotiations. 'Ibe greed!' he shouted rudely.

'Don't you worry about that dear. Lots of our clients have that
trouble but it doesn't last long. Now, did you say you were
British?'

Joseph gave up. 'Ibe Briddish,' he said with a germy sigh.

'You have a funny accent. I can't seem to place it for the
moment.

'I hab a code.'

'Pardon?'

'*Code*!' he screamed between coughs.

'I see. We have just the thing for you.'

'There'd a bug goig aboud.'

'Yes, I expect they do. Well, down to haha business. Our fee is
two pounds for the interview, ancillary charges— depending on
your placing of course. Will you want to see one of our special-
ists?'

'You are Rooby Toolbogs I presube?'

'Pardon?'

'*Rooby Toolbogs*!'

'Roomy Toolbox? Yes, that's our professional advertisement.'

'Well thed, wad id all thid crab aboud idderviewd and spedi-
ahd? All I wad id a sibble bang.'

'We can talk about all that when you arrive.'

'Ibe norbal, you know. You dode hab do ged oud the Alsatiod
for be, you dig?'

'Our address is 33 Princes Drive—you know how to get there?'

84

'Yed.'

'Bye-bye now.'

'Yed.' Joseph hung up and replaced the wet receiver in its cradle. He stuck a cigarette in his mouth and lit it. It tasted like a fog with pins in it and started him barking again. He pinched off the end with a practiced parsimony and put it back in the packet. In the street he crammed a handful of cough lozenges into his mouth as he hastened, lust-ridden, to his tryst via the 27 red, no change. Joseph Clark, no E.

'We've got a funny one tonight,' the madam told her girls. 'I can't make out what he wants.'

'Kinky?' asked the redhead.

'Coo, I should say so. He kept rabbiting on about Alsatians and governesses and going round bugs. I gather he's green and frigid.'

'Frigid?'

'Cold, he said. So was Christie. You'd better keep an eye on him. We don't want any more trilbies in the lavatory.

So when Joseph arrived, practically pole-vaulting in through the door, he found himself assigned to the biggest, fattest, most adaptable specialist in the house, a lady nominated in her absence and at present buying rock and chips twice at the corner shop.

The madam showed him up to her room to wait, rejoicing in his pigment — spades went on so and went back to her telly, Panorama, with a lighter heart. Joseph had never been to a brothel before and going up the stairs, fuelled his fires with reflection like *So this is a brothel* and *I'm in this brothel, then*, while outwardly he affected a jaunty ease. On the bus he had imagined their conversation 'You'd better use something because I can't — RC, you dig. You don't want to take chances with me.' The danger was delicious and the thought of scattering seed, like fivers, into the wind, made him feel swashbuckling and affluent.

The bedroom door closed behind him and he stared with growing de-tumescence at the deployment of peculiar instruments on the coffee table. Some purposes he divined — whips, boots, handcuffs: some purposes were murky but just possible — bicycle tyres, oilskin hats: two things, purposeless and frightening, really hung him up and set the old frontals reeling. Nine jars of Vick and a stuffed cat. Not that Vick and stuffed cats turned his knees to water — some of his best friends and that — it was the context that harrowed. What the hell could you do with them — here? The possibilities made him cough. The stuffed cat glared at him from glass eyes. Its mouth was open wide and he could see into its red painted throat. It stood upright on the bedside table holding, in that clumsy way that cats have, and silently playing, a large gilt harp. Joseph went closer to inspect it by the intimate twilight of the brocade lamp. Close, it was worse. 'Chride! Ibe geddig oud. Fug thid for a gabe of skiddles,' moaned Joseph, with a twitch of the sphincter.

He started for the door, thinking feverishly for an excuse, finding none and meanwhile dabbing down the landing, boots in hand, leaving sweat marks on the lino. At the top of the stairs he heard a sound below and froze. The lavatory yawned vacantly, he flitted in, a muffled moth in his woollies, and hide behind the door. He held his breath as footsteps clacked by and a smell of chips wafted past this mute, inglorious Bisto Kid's smeller. Versatile, he breathed through his mouth, went hot and cold and listened. The steps slowly returned.

And then he coughed. Coughed with the clangour of playground cops and robbers.

The door was pushed with force enough to stamp *Wash Your Hands, Please* on his seat.

'Come out from behind the door! Come on!' roared the biggest fattest specialist in the house. 'I'll have your guts for garters.'

'I card you twerb. Youb god be wedged!'

A large arm came into view, groping like a fun palace prizepicker and won Joseph, who felt himself roar into view, lacking only a cellophane bow.

'What were you doing in there, might I ask?' she did ask.

'I wad taked shord,' replied Joseph.

'Oh yes? We've heard that one before. We know what you get up to in there. And where's your hat?'

'I didn't wear id. Sdraw wend soggy in the raid lard nide.'

'You sure it was in the rain?' She muscled him aside and peered into the lavatory bowl.

'Wod you lookig in the bog for? God barby hab you?'

'Kinky, that's what. My room is the place for that sort of filth, not the toilet.

She herded him along the landing, he pulling on his boots as he went, hopping, graceful as a kick-start, and wiltingly into her boudoir. She closed the door and stared at him.

'I shall be very cross if I catch you skulking in my toilet again. It's no good for you. You know what happens to naughty boys.' She gave an arch look, licking vinegar from her thumb. Joseph sniffed powerfully to show he'd been around. Nobody panicked.

'Wod?' he asked petulantly.

'Naughty boys get smack bums.'

'Loog. I dode wad a smack bub. Ibe nod a poove, Bissis.'

'You asked for the governess on the phone so that's what you're getting. We haven't got any Alsatians so you'll have to make do.'

'I nebber asked for a fubbig gubberdess — I…'

'Ooh! Listen to him. Wash your mouth out with soap.'

'Nebber.'

'Well, what do you want then. You want to browse through the menu or what?'

Haughtily Joseph sniffed an errant candle back up into its lair. 'Ibe norbal. I cabe here for a draightforward ride' — he noticed the tyre — 'an ordinary fug. Nobody seebs to dough wad Ibe talkig aboud. Call thid a brothel — id a bloody wax-workd.'

'Oh is *that* it — she told me all wrong. You've never done it before luv and you were a bit nervy on the phone. You want me to coax you, I know all about it.'

She swarmed all over defiant Joseph — 'Ibe changed by bind' — and elbowed him playfully into the armchair, stroking fingers depleting his studies of at least *Das Kapital* in the hardback.

'Eh ere!' he protested, grabbing abortively at his money.

'Removes embarrassment, luv,' she said. 'Now you can just relax and pretend I'm your little lady friend. Now take off your little coat.'

'Dough I hab a heaby code. I keep id ode.'

'Come on, don't be shy.' She tugged at his mock mohair. Joseph twisted away and slapped at her hands.

'Off id!' he shouted. 'Greasy, fishy figgers off by obercoad. Cost boney, you dough.' She released him and stood up. 'I tage id off when Ibe ready. Dot before.'

'Don't be shy — look I'm taking off' — fingers unbuttoning — '*all* my clothes.' Huge breasts flopped red and white 'I don't know what's come — ZIP, skirt falls — 'over me' — big fat thighs lolled over stocking tops in a jungle of black suspenders slung low for a speedy draw. She advanced a pitted thigh, and slowly turned her hanging packet of buttocks towards him for his delectation. Her calves looked like boiled eggs in her cupping red bootees. Joseph looked hard and long at this mountain of lady, but he wouldn't pretend she was just his little girlfriend and his unease remained. He had never felt less lustful. He thought suddenly of representing his visit as an official CP feeler, but decided not to until he had unravelled the Kulak angle.

The cat glared at him from its harp, strung with a brother — a client? — as she moved, faith-powered, on her leather turntable. 'Oh dear,' she said, knickers descending, 'I seem to be losing my tight little scanties.'

She hid only her giggly face behind a pudgy fan of fingers, eyes darting fire and challenge at the sniffling swain. The whole works swished into view.

I'm not going in there, thought Joseph, and said 'Wod thad moggy for?'

'Naughty man. That's my little pussy,' she coyly buffed at her muff.

'Wod id for?'

'Don't you know? I should have thought a big boy like you would know.'

'Well, I dode.'

'Naughty tease — I know you only want to hear me say it.'

'Thad why I'be askig, thicky. Wod you want with a mangy old thig like thad. I should thing id be full of flead.'

Scarlet, she flailed at him, a meaty whack hurled him into the slips. In shock, both nostrils popped and he smelt for the first time the heady brew of chips and talcum. 'Bastard !' she screamed, barging him into the bedside table. The cat fell onto the carpet and began to pluck the harp, a plangent *Blue Danube*, turning its head on every fourth bar to mew from frozen mouth at popeyed Joseph.

'Whiskers,' she sobbed, running. 'Mummy's coming.'

'Daddy's off!' Joseph cried, sprinting, scooping up money and Vick as pour-boire and pour-chest. 'Thangs for nothig.'

6

The laudable moral recovery of Dr Ostbahn owed its origin to fear, its termination to death, and it occupied the space of two weeks in his life. It formed a coda at the end of his life, a coda based on thematic material; encapsulated, recapitulant. All his life he had been tired and afraid; both now reached such a pitch in intensity that had he not been murdered he would have died of them.

His heart was weak due to a pneumonic condition dating from his boyhood when, tired as since and with an incredible lack of cran, he had fallen asleep during a snowball fight at scout camp in Austria. At this same date he had added fear to his characteristics, a fear that grew quieter as the years passed and he remained alive, but that never left him. Of late an equable relationship had grown between the enemy within and the tired doctor, like that between chess adversaries of long standing, so that when a sudden attack sent him reeling into the wall, he would pat his chest and smile and say wryly, 'Aha — mein old familiar.'

'Take it easy,' said the specialist, 'you've got to take it steady.' For Otto Ostbahn this was the *wendepunkt*, the big light on the Damascus road, and paradoxically his moral decline followed it. He took it easy throughout the World Wars, yawning through both and dicing with death only during the Great Pumpernickel Craze, when he overate. Moral attitudes were for the bell-sound; for him life was a dummy run. Only when taking it easy had brought him safely to sixty-five, with a faded wife, and an ebbing practice did Ben appear and apply the electrodes.

Sitting with his collar off before the television he mentally added the six five-pounds he had earned that week for phone calls to the proper channels, and deducted the frisson caused by the policeman with ingrowing toenails. The doctor felt he had come out of it on the profit side. Yes, it might turn out for the best after all. He yawned and turned his attention to the screen.

'Heildelberg,' he said.

'Heildelberg,' said the quizmaster.

'Very clever, dear,' said Mrs Ostbahn, looking up from her knitting. The programme ended and he rose and switched off the set. He remained standing for a while gazing off into space. Mrs Ostbahn knew that he would now ask her for the paper but she waited for him to say it, because she was a frugal wife and knew how to husband their relationship. Meanwhile she kept an eager, ready for anything expression on her face and unravelled a new ball of wool.

'Have you seen the paper?' he asked.

Her eyebrows rose. 'Why yes, dear. I'm sitting on it.' She gathered the knitting into one hand and heaving a buttock off the chair, scooped beneath her and produced it.

'Anything in it?'

Now she frowned and placed a finger on her cheek in token of thought. She always omitted international affairs, politics, opinion, sport, articles, reviews, astrology and the cartoons because her husband had no interest in any of them.

'Oh yes. There's a girl who miscarried on page three. The police seem to think there was something not quite nice about it. Column two, dear.'

Dr Ostbahn shook the paper open and started to read. Under the liner *Police do not rule out quackery* an account was given of a twenty-year-old unmarried girl who was admitted to St George's Hospital that morning with an internal haemorrhage from which she had since died. She had made no statement but the police believed she had been the victim of an illegal operation.

'Why do you always have to crumple the paper like this?' he shouted at his wife, and thus began the laudable moral recovery of Dr Ostbahn. He could not rest until he had searched through his list of patients for the girl's name and he couldn't rest when he found it wasn't there. After a sleepless night he hammered downstairs at seven to see if the morning papers had arrived. From his surgery he phoned the number Ben had given him but there was no reply, and the words he had bravely prepared to terminate their partnership stayed with him, buzzing in his head. He was hooked but he couldn't find the man holding the line. 'A new leaf,' he muttered as he dusted at his desktop and bore a sea of tatty periodicals before him to the dustbin, past the amazed receptionist.

'Phone for a cleaner, miss,' he shouted, red with exertion, 'and I want her now. Today.' Then he put his head round the door again. 'And from now on I want you here every day. I pay you for every day. Monthlies arrive monthly, not twice a week on Mondays and Fridays. It is in their nature and conveyed in their name, monthlies. So we will have no more of it. And don't chew gum.'

The new Ostbahn didn't catch on. His wife cried in secret and the receptionist swore. 'He's gone on his drugs,' said Mrs Palmer, an elderly hypochondriac, smarting under his crisp demands for more coherent symptoms than 'funny'. The patients left to him after thirty years of inertia, had been pruned down to the hysterical — who leaned on his calm disinterest, the bored — who came to talk, and a shifting clientele of individuals who were actually sick enough to blunder in off the streets, win a note to a specialist and blunder out again. None of them were gassed by the new image, and high among the ungassed were the pregnant girls who were now informed that he knew no telephone numbers and definitely would not jab their buttocks with his hypodermic.

He spent a day reading his old university notes until the evening papers came, by which time he had realised that whatever else he had become in the years since graduation, he had not become a doctor of medicine. And now it was too late. He tried the phone again and heard the endless rise and fall of bells within walls he had never seen, did not need to see to know that they held his freedom and that the hook in his brain was held or had been held by the occupant of those walls. Joseph Narodniki. He paced his surgery and jangled the change in his pockets and then went out again. In the street the idea came to him that he could find his silent partner if he tapped the resources of the twentieth century. Of course. What a useless fool he had been! He would become a private detective.

Armed with the phone book for the city area and a ruler, he slid his eye down the number listings. The task could have taken weeks but Dr Ostbahn was lucky. Five pages in, he found what he wanted.

Joseph's door lolled open, his name printed on the card under the drawing pin, but Joseph was out. The doctor, wheezing from his climb, stared for a long time at the phone on the wall outside. It stood on a little shelf all by itself like a deity, an icon. Was this what he had been looking for? On the wall in its immediate vicinity were cabalistic markings. He put on his reading glasses and read the list of cinemas, record shops and addresses in Joseph's fast flat fist. Among the aimless doodles of saxophones and quavers was his own phone number. He took out his pencil and with the eraser nub removed himself from the company; he copied down the other numbers into his diary and thus bequeathed a puzzle the equal of the *Marie Celeste* to his subsequent biographers at the police station.

The empty room diverted him for a full hour. Joseph had left a fascinating effluvium to the nosy, a rich skimming from the cream of his personality. The doctor pounced on the packing of a new shirt and read the trade name: *Brute*. Very appropriate! Under the shirts, the drawers were lined with old *Melody Maker*s and *Tribune*s, a dead fly and a broken cufflink; in the fireplace he found a solid newspaper of fish and chips. And then he found it, Joseph's shameful secret, a little book concealed among his record covers, its title *Hip Words*. The doctor recognised some of the hip words from Ben Herod; that made it a clue. Joseph Clark was possibly Joseph Narodniki, henchman of Ben Herod. But he didn't find who held the hook.

'I wish to place an advertisement in the *Mail*.'

'Right ho, sir. Print the message on this form.' The pushed a biro into his hand. 'And it's six shillings a line.' The clerk read it aloud. 'That's it, is it?'

The doctor felt his heart swell until it touched the walls of his body. He stood very still, scarcely daring to breathe, waiting for the spasm to pass. Surely the message was too obvious? Everyone, this clerk, every Mail subscriber would know exactly who Mr Herod was. Why had he chosen such a stupidly obvious name? It was not too late to snatch it back and destroy it. He shot an agitated look at the clerk. The paper lay on the counter between his hands and the clerk was staring vacantly over the doctor's shoulder at the people passing in the street outside. He suspected nothing, the doctor was sure of that. He must go through with it because it was the only course of action that lay open to him. Only by finding the abortionist could he get off the hook. He would offer him a hundred pounds for the tape-recording and because the man was greedy he would take it. He would buy back his reputation, refuse to rent the honourable shelter of the medical profession to a quack who probably didn't even wash his hands before choking the baby in the womb.

'Yes. That is all,' he replied firmly.

Ben came out of the *Mail* offices at two o'clock the following day and Dr Ostbahn fell into step fifty yards behind him. The doctor had taken great care over his plan. He wore an overcoat that his wife had tried to throw out two winters ago and which even now bore the smell, bonfires, of a near miss. Only a fraction of his face was discernible between the pulled up collar and the pulled down hat, purchased yesterday. He wore Trotsky glasses and a khaki haversack. A great many people turned round to look at him as he passed. Every time Ben turned a corner and swung for an instant into profile, the doctor galvanised into a limp so complex and handicapping that had Ben lived any further from the *Mail* offices, he would have lost him.

He saw Ben disappear into a large, crumbling Victorian house, the first house off the main road. The doctor licked his lips. Now he had him the man who held the hook. Radiant with malice, the private eye went home to wait for the evening edition.

The paperboy flexed new waxed biceps and handed the mighty order, two national evenings, a county, a weekly and a local, to Mrs Ostbahn who, strong on teamwork, handed to snatching spouse at her elbow. Under the legend *Personal Ads* he found what he sought. There was eighteen shillings worth:

CATCH OSTBAHN'S LATEST HIT SINGLE
THE MOTHERS' LAMENT
ON THE FLIP — THE NEEDLEWORK SONG.

Sixteen teenagers drew a blank at their local disc-centre and the tiny tremor registered on the national charts to be forgotten, along with the number one, in a week. The ad ran for three nights and the coffee bars buzzed with the name of the old German doctor.

Dr Ostbahn was a square. He wished to God and back that he had never cut his single and prayed to Him that it never became a hit. Also, for the first time, he seriously entertained the idea of going to the police, telling all and taking his punishment like a fearless Queen's Evidence. He would be ruined but he would take his tormentor with him. The more he thought about that, the better he felt. If Ben had the hook in him, he had the hook in Ben, and now by facing up to his guilt he had gained a position of strength to bargain from; best of all, he didn't have to go to the police unless the proposed *détente* failed to take.

But Ben was out, had been out for several days and the newspaperman outside, who seemed to live there, did not know when or if he would be back. The doctor gave him a day, then two days, then three and at last played his penultimate counter. It took the form of two words in the *Mail*:

HEROD. POLICE.

This turned out to be his ultimate counter.

7

Jenny, feeling sick, fixed her mind on the richness of opportunity ahead. She lay half-propped amid pillows on the bed and carefully hiccoughed a vodka hiccough. So what was this 'ere richness of opportunity? To go on as they were? More parties, more clothes, more doing what they liked and when? And how! She couldn't see that Billy would alter his life or that she would alter it for him. What had happened after the last time? For a week he had saved money and devised the future; what people did when planning for a baby, he did after losing it; and then stopped. So they'd go on as they were. This, the here and now, was the price: here, now, why this man, this professional was methodically wiping each instrument on a white towel and replacing them in their box: why Billy was sitting a mile away in the Swan blotting up whisky and exuding sweaty fear. And she could afford it, both the fear and the pain, regretting only, despite logic, despite time, the child-shaped blank spreading its spatial memory through the guts.

Nausea spun the room around her and the man unravelled into a multiplication of outlines away from the black parent figure. When it passed she saw that he was at the sink coiling red rubber tube into the water and cleaning it. He did this with the utmost concentration and, watching, she knew she would feel nothing until he had finished, could feel no pain until he turned that incredible concentration to her.

Of course it took guts to get rid of it. Billy never stopped explaining this to people. You needed all those capitals — Courage, Decision, Strength of Purpose — to enjoy your life, qualities that people applauded in war, urged on sons of widowed mothers, and admired in careers. The pursuit of happiness took an iron man. Most people cracked under the responsibility of not holding down a job and a house, capitulated and threw up a palisade of babies to live for instead. And Billy was right.

'I can't bear to see you in pain,' he had said behind a Christ face, so she had given him a pound and a kiss and sent him off to the pub. So what? She didn't live with Billy for his strength or his reliability or even for his lovemaking. Jenny could make a list like Magna Carta of what she didn't live with Billy for. He wasn't even faithful, but that was all right: when he was with her he had her, and when he was away he had someone else. He always told her about it and he made her laugh until her head ached. That was what he had. Billy had words that changed your way of seeing until everything became funny as hell and quick and jerky like the Keystone Cops, and you could see all the mess and uncertainty disappeared into whimsical little parcels. Billy was just a fact and she knew him better than she would ever know anyone. Even this would be funny. When he came back from the pub he would put his head on her breast and stroke his hair until he was himself again, because if he wasn't funny there wasn't anything else he was. Then she would hand him this afternoon of pain and fear and he would rewrite it.

Jenny looked at the man, the professional, leaning against the wall, staring out of the window and smoking, completely contained, completely unassailable, and knew that soon he would become for her a sort of bungling, forelock-tugging plumber. But she wouldn't tell Billy everything because he couldn't use everything and if it broke him, it broke her. She would leave out the bit about the man demanding and taking her body when she was frantic with fear and drink and imposing a peace on her so that she felt good, wonderful, before the pain. Or for the pain? A nasty thought. Did he enjoy springing his seed before the avalanche: into the void, on to the eraser? She didn't know and she wouldn't ask. It had the Pill whacked all ends up. Then again, had it been done for her? To calm her? To establish an intimacy for their collaboration in the most basic way open to the species?

If that was his aim he had achieved it, because here too he was a professional, unlike Billy, but unlike Billy he wasn't a person.

She moved her legs stiffly so as not to dislodge the folded wedge of towels at her groin. 'An elephant's jamdam,' Billy had said last time.

'How do you feel?' His hand gently rested on her brow.

'I feel — sort of waiting very hard. Leaning into it though it isn't there yet.'

'No pains?'

'No.'

He stroked her damp hair back from her forehead but she shook away.

'No, it's meant to be like that. It's supposed to be a carefree fringe. Billy cut it that way.' She removed a bare arm from the sheets and brushed her hair forward again.

'That's how he sees you?'

'That's how he sees me.'

'Does he know there's more?'

'More?'

'More to you.'

'He sees what he likes to see.'

'Uh huh.'

They smiled over absent gulping Billy.

'You're very good at your job.'

'I'm the best.'

'I've been done before you know. I'm qualified to pass an opinion.'

'You said.' He lit a cigarette from his and put it between her lips.

'He was hopeless. I had to go to hospital and of course they were very helpful and tried to save it. I told them I had fallen downstairs but I could see they didn't believe me. Not much they could do about it though. Anyway I was all right, I lost it and after a bit they sent me home. Anyway — oh yes — your colleague. He kept on bending over to look — you know, look up there. I don't know what he thought he could see. I mean I'm not illuminated. And he kept on saying "They could put me away for this, lady" and getting in a flap.'

Jenny assumed a throaty voice 'Gawd, I've left me hat inside,' but she knew that Billy did it better. When she tried to remember the first time, she couldn't. All she got was Billy's version and sometimes a picture of flesh staked hack with pins that had also never happened, but came with the word abortion. How long would she remember this moment, these hands stroking her forehead as they had stroked her thighs before the greased red tube slid in and he had made his strike.

The man went over to the sink and put the enamel bucket she had dug out for the occasion under the tap, rinsed it and poured in a little disinfectant. She noticed the bottle of vodka on the glass shelf above the sink still half-full, he had not touched a drop, alien among the tooth brushes and talcums of everyday.

'You wouldn't let me off the money,' she said, just to probe his concentration. He finished the job without speaking or giving any indication that he had heard. Then he dried his hands.

'Nope,' he said.

'I didn't think you would.' He smiled and lit another cigarette.

'You smoke too much.'

'Too much for what?'

'For your health.'

'Smoking is good for you.'

'Would you give me a rebate for the free ride?' She felt bolder now, watching him from her impregnable invalid's bed.

'I don't charge for the ride. That was free. You got that for appearance.

'Thanks a lot.' She felt her stomach heave and drew her legs up around the sudden pain. 'How did you learn this fine art?'

'I held the midwife's bike-clips.'

'You don't have to stay with me.'

'You want me to fade?'

'No,' she said, clutching his hand, 'not at that price.'

8

As they entered the almost deserted university Joseph turned his worried face to John and said: 'John, what do you know about the Kulaks?'

'Nothing. Sod all.'

'Where would I look then?'

John looked at him incredulously, so Joseph set off a smoke-screen.

'Test me on History. Go on man — ask me anything.' Joseph sued his boon with a naive little push at John's front.

'Okay,' said John, 'what do you know about Henry VII?'

'Everything man,' said Joseph. 'Ask me something specific.'

He was bouncing around on his toes like a boxer in training and snapping his fingers.

'Okay,' said John, starting to walk again, 'how did he make himself secure on the throne?'

'*Bam*! Two things bugged Henry when he got on the stand. 1485 man. One: he was strictly from the sticks — Mr Zero from Nilville. He had this chickencrud claim through the Clerk of the Wardrobe, Owen Chuder. Like he was only keeper of the royal threads but he managed to slip French Kate a length and that put the Chuder show on the road. Anyway, no-one had big eyes for Henry so he had to like bear down with his personality and make a big production of having God in his corner. And he made sure his court was where it was at, for, you know, for the Fifteenth

Century. It featured all the noble cats of the time all in sharp threads man, and Henry seat at the top. He made sure everybody could see he was King of Hip Castle.'

'What about the nobility?' John asked, squinting into the wind.

'Strictly defunct, man. No scene any more. Do you mind stopping — I can't walk and coach man. All the real rockers got theirs in the Wars of the Roses and Henry really put the arm on the remains at Bosworth. Then he called a cool and to make sure it took he got the Fuzz — the Chuder Fuzz was called JPs see — he got the Fuzz to collect all their blades and pieces so they couldn't bop if they felt like it. Then he put a big tax on the liveried muscle to liquidate their gangs.

'What was the second thing that bugged him?'

'I was coming to that. Henry was broke like he was really hurting for money. He even owed for out of town help in the Bosworth rumble. But now he's King see, so his worries are over. When you've made it it's easy to get some action cash-wise, it's all there. All you've got to do is turn the handle like playing the fruit machines. He makes this royal decree they've all got to lay their bread on him and it starts rolling in. He makes a heap on sheep — sheep go like grease on the market — like the Dutch use them for threads. Then there's customs. Baby, whatever moves in or out he gets a slice of the action. He draws protection because he's Number One in the goddam realm. It's all his turf. Everybody has to shell out and I tell you, he ain't taking no wooden tally sticks. The groats start rolling in.'

Despite the discomfort of just standing there in the freezing wind, John was fascinated. The small animated figure in front of him exploded in all directions, arms waving to emphasise a point then hurled up to anchor the inevitable hat, feet chattering out a tempo for the words. He looked like a badly pegged tent in a hurricane.

'Why didn't all the previous kings get rich then? If it was all there?'

'Simple. The rockers took it. They was bent as hell, always cooking the books, stacking the pack. But Henry wasn't going to take that kind of crap. He lamps the books man and he sez : "This is a helluva note. You think I'm simple or something? From here on in, I'm taking over accounts and you cats can go play with yourselves. Paste that in your visors."'

'Does the cool take?'

'It takes time. He hitches up with this Yorkist chick to show the cool is for real but the rockers start putting up pretenders. First there's this guy Lambert Simnel. He's just a dummy but the rockers put out this story he's one of the princes in the Tower. Natch Henry's hip to this angle. He knows these princes got turned off with a pillow by Hatchetman Tyrrel, so he figures it for a switch. Henry catches him — no strain at all. He doesn't even bother to kill him — this Simnel is just a fall guy see, just a dummy. Henry puts him in the royal kitchen throwing hash from sunup to sundown, so that's all right.'

Joseph seemed to have paused for breath. He frowned in irritation; for him, speed was merit and if you hung up you flopped. He had the greatest memory he had ever encountered and always cursed the faculty to hell for not giving oral exams, for not letting you smoke and for setting snide correlation questions. He lit a match in his hat and applied it to a fag. 'Ask me anything,' he said, putting his hat back into place.

John couldn't think of anything to ask. 'Did he like it there?' he said at last.

'What? Where?'

'In the royal kitchen?'

'How the hell should I know? I didn't write this stuff you know. Some old scribe did. You think he was going to say "I wunner if I should say he liked it there?" You think he was gonna worry himself about some Chuder counter-jerk?'

'You seem to know it pretty well,' said John placatingly.

'I've learnt it all up. Ask me anything.'

'No. I believe you. It's okay.'

'I'll tell you about Canute and the Surfing Set?' Joseph offered, trotting along beside him again.

'No don't tell me any more Joseph — it confuses me.'

Joseph tightened his lips and raised his eyebrows. He was insulted. 'Sod you then. I thought I made it pretty clear.'

'Yes yes, you did but – I'm slower than you. I have to go over it.'

Joseph's sharp ears heard the note of appeasement and at once. Pity he didn't know about the Kulaks though.

They had reached the library by now, a huge box of concrete and tin emblazoned with an emblematic owl in leftover lumps of cement. Builders huts and a prefabricated bicycle shed flanked them and their boots slid over frozen mud.

'I'll see you at the pub at one. I've got to do some work first. Here, read this.' John gave him a brand new *Jazz Monthly* to get rid of him.

'Okay,' said Joseph. 'I'll see you in the bar at one. Hang loose, dad.' He gave his Indian sign and bobbed off into the distance, one hand on his hat, the other holding the magazine in a convenient reading position.

John sighed and went in.

The enormous door closed behind him with a carpet-slipper farty sound — *pfff* — a sound to go with the hot canned air which now enveloped him. It was like, he thought, stepping into a tropical jungle. The book-stamper was thumping through a pile of books on the centre desk as if reading music. She produced three rhythmic timbres — the tap of book cover on the wooden desk; the deep whump of the rubber date-stamp; the pneumatic bump of cover descending on pages. Behind her flashing, bespectacled head he saw the dark grille of the taboo bookcase. At the desk he made a magic hand-painting in perspiration and laid down the books he was carrying.

'Can I check these in?' he asked, flipping them open at the date-card and intruding a double tap into her motif.

The stamper, a thirty-year-old lump in a forty-year-old Fair Isle cardigan with a bobbled zipper, flashed her glasses purposefully up at him and then down to the books. She set down her rubber stamp on an inked pad.

'You realise these are two months overdue?' she shrieked as if there were a bushfire in her drawers.

John fished out a crumpled ten shilling note and laid it beside the books. He thought it a pity that Carol could never see money as anything but filthy because it meant someone else had to stump up. The stamper ignored the money and continued to inspect the books, both volumes of Byron.

'Look at this! Disgraceful!' Her glasses wildly hurled prisms, neon splinters, aluminium at him. 'Damaged! The pages have been ripped loose of the binding! The frontispiece has gone too!'

The head librarian, who was apathetically piddling about with the filing cabinets, buttoned his leather-elbowed Harris and strode to the desk.

'What's the trouble?' he asked, hoping it was lots as business was slack, donning donnish frown that rattled back in corrugations over pink pate. The stamper's chair uttered a parakeet screech on the lino as she leaped up to thrust her defenceless femininity at the gaunt figure of her superior.

'Oh Mr Gorr! He's brought these books back two months overdue — not a word of apology of course — and this one has been torn away from its spine — it looks as if he's thrown it across the room and jumped on it. And this one has been rubbed in grass or something. Look at the state of the flyleaf! And to finish it off he's torn out Byron's frontispiece!'

The head librarian flung John an anchoring glare, the mixture: foreboding and malice, equal parts. He presented his dome as he assessed the raped and overdue on the desk. The sward marks were undeniable.

John could appreciate the snapping tension. A dreadful hush fell on the library, a hush the worse for the sinister creak of Mr Gorr's spectacles as frowns buckled his averted features. Now and then, in the distance, John could hear the metallic thud of head slumping hopeless to desk.

The head librarian held the pages by their veriest tips, suggestive both of repugnance and of his own irreproachable reading method, and launched a ticking sound of little melodic interest. The stamper in the jumper was swift to add body to his ticking with deep heavy sighs, laden — she postulated with cinnamon and with myrrh. His nearside pane fogged. Their fingers bumped.

'Could I possibly have your attention?' asked the librarian nastily. He held up a dry russet leaf and a feather. 'Can you explain these?'

'They're a leaf and a feather.' That was an easy one.

'That's patently obvious. One knows what they are. The question is, can you explain their presence in this volume? If you please.'

John smiled. He could see her pressing them into the book with love and reverence and of course forgetting them. He didn't mind all this fuss, he may as well be here as anywhere else, but he vaguely wished she were here to return her own books and turn the blade of the interrogation, with the tranquil gaze of the natural, into a consciousness for Mr Gorr of his rude and heinous materialism. Can any human being, Mr Gorr, read Byron without emotion? See how the crumpled page bore witness to her fury at man's inhumanity to man, this blotch, a tear drawn forth for the wandering outcast of his own dark mind. Joseph had

nicked the frontispiece for Byron's shirt, a floppy flexroll number, reproducible, the tailor told him, for three quid.

'No,' said John.

'Give me your name,' said the librarian producing a pen filled
with Zyklon B.

'Jenkins, J,' said John, nothing loth.

'Faculty?'

'History finalist.'

'I see.' He wrote down all this biography, the titles of books,
the extent of the damage, and then zoned in the stamper and her
stamp with a pointing finger. 'You realise that as a member of this
library you have been hitherto regarded as a civilised person,
and that all books loaned to you were loaned in that belief. On
trust, in short.'

'I do,' said John groomily.

'You fully appreciate that these works are on the English
finals syllabus, and that by seeing fit to withhold them from cir-
culation you have jeopardised the chances of some candidates in
their examinations. Does this strike you as civilised behaviour?'

'Yes, No,' said John.

The head librarian's voice, hitherto in the style Deceptively
Mild now rang forth roundly as he sprung his trap: 'Then why
didn't you return them in January?'

John observed the unmistakable sense of drama in their
demeanour; he, radiant with malice, his features cocked above
irreproachable county check, waited; she, beside him, held the
accused in tiny bondage on her glasses; neither knew that John
loved above all things the waiting moment when activity con-
gealed and time was immeasurable. This was his moment
because he understood it, his alone because he could merge into
it doing nothing, for once, with relevance and success. So he
merely stood there and watched them realise their limbo.

'In January my father was ill with chicken pox,' said John
finally. Thus, spotting his father's memory, he rejoined the fray.
The librarian had lost heart. In a whisper he fell back on regula-
tions. 'Did you have the books cleared by an MO?'

'No,' said John.

'I see,' seeing Byron aswarm and rubbing his fingers together.

'They weren't in the house, see.'

'Oh?'

'No. I had them in hospital with me.'

Behind thick lenses the librarian's eyes mutely begged to be left in ignorance.

'Unidentified skin disease.'

'Of course you handled the books as much as possible.'

'No. It was too noisy to concentrate in the ward. I like peace when I read.' John leaned forward confidentially. 'I like reading in the lav best.'

A nervous trill escaped the stamper. Both stared at her. She flushed and began riffling through the ticket file. Suddenly her fingers stopped, her mouth contracted into an O, as in whistling but poutless. 'Mr Gorr!' she breathed, 'a terrible thing. The books were loaned to Miss Carol Scott.'

There was a moment of heavy silence.

'Then these aren't your books?'

'No,' said John, with a puzzled frown.

'You're only returning them I take it?'

'Oh yes.'

'You didn't damage them?'

'Afraid not.'

'You've deliberately wasted my time then!'

'Nobody asked me if they were my books. I naturally assumed that you'd checked the tickets first. I was quite surprised in fact. Still, don't worry about wasting my time — I wouldn't have been doing anything else. A bit of last minute revision perhaps. I can tell Miss Scott about jeopardising other students' chances and Byron's frontispiece and abusing the trust and so on, so you won't have to say it all again. Regard me as a sort of middleman.'

John got his money and walked softly away to the study cubicles. He felt curiously cheated of victory. His moment had been destroyed because he had been forced to initiate events, successfully it was true, but on their terms. Still, it made a funny story. He chose a History cubicle, choosing for lack of view and maximum neutrality. He had already lent out his magazine. He lowered himself into the chair. This was to be it. Work. He stared at the blank pad before him on the desk and then wrote: *Henry VII*. He drew a line under this, utilising the straight edge of his text-book and a red biro, and then, frowning added: *Tudor*. He drew a line under that too.

Covering his face in sudden despair, he fought to see the warp and woof of it all. God what shit it all was! Couldn't they see how absurd the bloody subject was? Sixty-odd pages of *Henry VII* and no-one knew what he was like. Joseph's interpretation was the only one possible, to hoover the dust off the archive and use his own words to make it his. Among all those facts, councils, proclamations, institutions, conspiracies, marriages, not one of these proper students of mankind had touched the man. How did Henry's life seem to Henry?

John gazed at the small square of sky visible through the high window. What went through that antique Tudor bonse when he saw that same grey scudding sky? No-one knew because no-one could know. So what's it all about, Alfie?

John's life was eighty per cent incoherence; an itch in the crutch, half a thought rising, evaporating, a colour glimpsed, the etiolated scar of an old fear: indescribable. Old Henry's must have been the same. So must, he thought, his father's. The finalist historian had lived for twenty years with that old man, spoken with him every day, bore his mark. He knew nothing about him. He even made things up about him — like the hot cock he had sold Carol about his endless manicuring and barbering. Sydney Jenkins: the Man and the Thinker. He could sit down at this massive archive of letters, diaries, photos, relatives, workmates and memories and sift it, select it, correlate, vacuum the turn-ups, pursuing an overall pattern, a central strand. That way he would lose the eighty per cent. He might even find the strand, rosebud, but Sydney Jenkins hadn't.

John shook these thoughts from his mind. He found this serial form mourning very wearing and his musings derivative. He took up his biro and wrote:

THE STRAIGHT DOPE FROM THE INSIDER
Scuttlebutt has it that this year's examiners are description buffs. Insider tips the following:
1 (a). An evocation of Nantes.
2. Who was the Great Seal?
2 (a). A day in the life of a groat.
CAUTION! Do not read more than both sides of the paper.
Do not pass GO.
(This will clock up the marks for you!)

He left the paper on the desk as an inspiration to others and quietly left the hall of learning to a handful of Ghanaians, who worked on to the rhythmic pulse of the book-stamper.

9

Carol sat on the station bench and watched pale moths bump around the lamp. She had been gazing at them for the last half-hour; they were having lots of fun. Beyond the lamp the night sky was a thick purple, cracked and splintered by the shapes of the trees. In the perfect stillness she could hear her heart thumping. Suddenly the platform clock made a noise — clonk. She stared, her eyes jumped to the hands and her consciousness everted to receive her surroundings. It was the first definite movement she had made in an hour.

She had raced up the road from the beach and into the empty station to find, finger sliding down the impossible runes of the timetable, that the next train would be tomorrow. And then, with the cold brass touch of the locked waiting-room door on her palm, she had stopped because there was nothing else she could do. All panic past, a strange mood of lethargy had settled upon her.

She got up now and started pacing about. *Come to Scarborough* said a Bathing Belle with a peewee moustache and flowmaster nipples like stalks on berets: she spoke in Granby Condensed.

Carol fixed her eyes on the unblinking red light at the end of the platform and walked towards it. The roof stopped short of the end, its edge crenellated like the jaw of a whale; Carol stepped out into the open on the concrete tongue of the ramp. The wind stirred her hair at her neck and hummed gently in the telegraph wires, but she felt too strange to write any of it down.

There were allotments to her left on the railway bank and she wondered in an alien gust of practicality whether she would find anything there to eat. She could dimly make out rows of knobbly cabbage stumps and on the skyline a palisade of bean poles hung with tinfoil and string. She remembered seeing lupins here last summer, pink and blue, and a scarecrow with silver railway-man's buttons that flashed in the sun. Pictures of still life for a hungry girl. Perhaps they kept iron rations in their sheds, hard-tack and chocolate at least? She was afraid to go and look. Sheds frightened her ever since the little boy next door had shown all in the shed in return for the same, and had poked a button into hers so that she peed in four streams for a day, until her mother detected the change of note and visited his mother. Carol had never felt under any of her subsequent lovers a fraction of that guilt: it was her first and last scrutiny of the mechanics of sex before the romance of it all closed over her mind like the Index.

When she turned away she was startled to see a man standing under the light, his back to her, putting a coin into the cigarette machine. Even as she thought, let him go away without seeing me, he turned and stared straight at her.

'Hi,' he called and just stood there as if waiting for the echo. Carol felt stupidly, obviously supplicant, her hands clasped in front of her around a volume of poetry.

'Hi,' she said, walking towards him with a jauntiness she did not feel.

'Missed the last train?'

'I think so.' She knew so.

The young man tore off the cellophane wrapper and stuck a cigarette in his mouth. 'Where do you want to be?'

'Hull?' Carol heard it slip out in a request, the edges curled up like a begging letter. She looked at his tie.

'Then I say "Do you want a lift?" And you say...'

She tried not to look as if she were assessing him, but her gaze lacked only a levelled pencil and a buckled eye.

He wore a dark suit, a dark overcoat, looked expensive like the lack of publicity bought for financiers. His face was bony with deep shadows under the cheekbones; if he filed his teeth it didn't show.

'So who looks their best in gaslight?' he said. 'It's a loaded set-up.' His gaze was direct, completely self-contained; it offered nothing. Carol nervously cleared her throat.

'I had a barrel round my neck but it got lost,' he said.

Carol smiled and tried to think of something to say.

'You're afraid of me?'

'Well,' she replied, 'I don't know you.'

He shrugged. 'I don't know me either.'

They were silent for a minute, Carol scuffing a circle in the dust with her shoe, he levelly watching her, waiting, smoking his cigarette without touching his hand to it.

'Well, I don't know,' said Carol at last.

'How do you feel about the Germans?'

'How do you mean?'

'Leaving that aside for a bit — which bugs you worse, rape or death? Or is it nameless? You spy with your little eye something beginning with a lift.' He flicked his fag-end onto the line. 'What you're looking for baby is Brown Owl driving a mini. You'd really like me to be a eunuch, right? Square.' Carol blushed.

'Blusher,' he said and suddenly grinned. 'Okay Credentials. The real warm well-documented me.' He undid his coat and reached into his pocket.

'Driving licence.' He slapped something down on the ticket counter and Carol saw that it was a folded handkerchief.

'Dog licence': a switch knife.

'Identity card': a pair of dark glasses.

He tried another pocket, his eyes never leaving her face.

'Birth certificate': a packet of Lucky Strike.

'Satisfied? Intellectually, I mean.' His hand hovered over his overcoat pocket like a gunfighter's.

'What's your name?' asked Carol.

'Ben Down.'

'I don't believe that.'

'Ben anyway to save you pointing. Come on.' He took her arm and she went with him. Her decision lay literally in his hands now. Somehow, she felt that he had presented, in spite of his words, a real picture of himself. He had refused to compromise; she could feel his integrity in the strong grip of his hand on her arm. She walked with him to his car.

Carol never noticed cars but she noticed this one. It was a dark green American convertible with a chrome fender like a mandarin's molars. It was about twenty feet long and it was all car. She hated it for most reasons but she got in when he opened the door for her.

'Quite a car,' she said, resenting the marshmallow seat that sighed up to pamper her posterior. 'Does it wake you up with a cup of tea in the morning?' She was always acid on technology.

'Yes,' said Ben, opened the glove compartment, almost disappeared inside, and handed her a thermos flask. 'Only it's coffee. The ethnic bit, you dig.'

'Are you American?'

'Sometimes.'

Carol poured out a plastic cupful of steaming coffee and drank. When it was all gone she closed her eyes and said: 'Ah.'

'Do you eat?' He produced a large bag of rolls and half a broiler chicken, and hefted them up and down in his hand.

'On your nose,' he said.

'Ben, I'm sorry I was rude,' said Carol, jettisoning about fifteen years in vocal development. 'But your car is a bit — overwhelming.'

'My one weakness. I could die of it.' Ben gave her the food, then watched her eat as if the process was somehow amazing. Not until she got to finger licking, without a net, did he turn away and start the car. The road unwound in the beam of the headlights, hedgerows and trees springing up ahead like stage flats.

'What do you do?' asked Carol, studying his profile.

'When?'

'Well, for a living.'

'Why's that?'

'Is it a mystery then?'

'Pardon?'

'A secret. Is what you do a secret?'

'Which do you want to know?'

'How, which?'

'Do you want to know if it's a mystery or a secret?'

'Um — is it — a mystery?'

'No, it isn't.'

'What do you do, then?'

'Do you mean "how do you do"?'

'No I don't. I mean what do you do?'

'Don't you want to know if it's a secret?'

'All right.'

'Ask me then.'

'Is it a secret?'

'No it isn't.'

'What is it then?'

'Ask me if it's something else.'

'I can't seem to care any more. I've gone off it,' Carol said, laughing. Ben turned his head round and thrust his tongue into his cheek making a bulge like a tent pole and then returned to profile. Carol giggled into her hand like a bashful geisha.

'What do you want to talk about then?' she asked him.

'I don't know.'

'Talk about what you like doing. Things you're interested in.'

'Like people do?'

'Yes.'

'Best of all I like sexual intercourse with ladies. Then second I dig thinking about it. Can you see your way clear to doing it with me?'

'I don't know you.'

'What do you have to know?'

'Well, a lot more than I know now.'

'Details?'

'What you do, what your name is, what you like doing…'

'You know all that.'

'What you believe in, what you were like as a boy, what sort of person you are…'

'You play all this back while the guys bounce up and down?'

'No, but knowing it gives me peace of mind afterwards. I have something of theirs.'

'Christ! Who have you been with?'

'That's a secret.' Carol suddenly saw herself as horribly set about with bourgeois rules of her own making; she had not been free at all. Prudent, cautious. The words were horrible. She couldn't face her own accusation so she made him the accuser and swung into her defence.

'Anyway, you haven't even asked my name.' She tilted her chin at him but he didn't look.

'I probably would have asked you but now I don't think I could bear the responsibility.' He didn't offer to explain or even indicate if this was a joke. 'I will ask you something though. Will anyone miss you if you don't get home?'

'What is that meant to mean?'

'You ain't got doll's ears.'

'I've got a big strong boyfriend. He'd miss me if I didn't get back tonight.'

'What was he like as a boy?'

'You're not very reassuring,' said Carol, wasting one of her short-sighted feminine looks on his profile.

'You don't want to be reassured.'

Carol saw the beach swing into view as they emerged from the lane and the car jounced on its springs as they ran onto sand. It was as empty and desolate as a desert.

'Ben! This is the beach. Ben!' She heard her voice quaver in proferring the widow's mite of his name, all she had against his menace. 'You can't get onto the road this way. It goes nowhere.'

Ben turned the car in a wide curve until they were moving parallel to the sea and about a yard from the water's edge. In the headlights the wet sand was the bright artificial colour of builders sand.

'Push that,' he said, pointing at the glowing green button on the dashboard.

'What will it do?' Carol was scared now: talk was talk but this was the beach: she was scared to touch anything.

'Oh come on. Push it for Ben.'

She put her forefinger on the button and leaned, her eyes fixed anxiously on him as if expecting manacles to snatch at her arms and him to X-ray horribly into a monster of teeth and sockets. The canvas hood rose in the air and slowly conecertina'd into a neat bundle over the boot; her relief was palpable.

The car sped shiningly between streams of sand and stars. She felt her body quieten now as the miles sped silently by, and she found herself smiling. Was he a romantic after all, a Sergeant Troy of the twentieth century paying his court with eye and wrist, with sinew and judgement, because that alone was true and clean? Ben, as if in answer to her thoughts, nudged the car into the shallows and zipped it through the flying spray like a lawn-mower. The twin headlights flung a misty rainbow over the sea.

Distance, measurement sank without trace between those eternal streams: nothing existed beyond the grasp of the head-lights, the drone of the engine. Carol closed her eyes and levitat-ed out of her mind. Faster they went and she shouted her deeper deepest swoopingly fallingly stuff into the slipstream, or only thought it, or was it. When at last the car glided to a halt she did not want to open her eyes. From a long way off she heard her mind tell her that this was it, but she didn't care. She was free. If he touches me I shall. If he takes my face between his hands.

Her eyes blinked open on the empty sea, on a trembling star above the tilted horizon. The driver's seat was empty.

'Ben?' she called.

He was leaning on her door studying her face. Spray hung in her hair; and she knew it.

'Do you want to do it?'

Carol turned away and began twisting a fold in her coat.

'Ben, you mustn't ask me,' she said quietly.

He opened the door. 'Get out,' he said.

The door clunked shut behind her, seemed to bite a wedge out of the night air, out of her body. She could smell the wind off the sea and she filled her lungs like a sail.

Ben took her hand and led her around the front of the car to the driving seat. She looked at him. She learned nothing from his face.

'Get in,' he said.

'I can't drive Ben.'

'You're joking.'

'No, it's true. I can't. I'm afraid.'

'Get in.'

She got in. Ben squatted down in the sand, his hands dangling loosely over his knees, his overcoat curtsying around him. Carol said nervously, 'You look like Toulouse Lautrec.'

'On the extreme right you'll find a pedal. That's the gas pedal. If you bear down on that the car will go faster, you dig? Now you know it all.'

'But Ben' — he got into the passenger seat beside her — 'I'm scared.'

He turned on the ignition and pulled the choke, and her foot, timidly resting on the accelerator, took off like a rocket as the engine roared into life.

'Don't go ape on the gas,' said Ben. 'You got another foot down there?'

Idiotically she nodded.

'Okay. Bring that other foot over towards me and push it down hard on the clutch pedal. Come on come on, squash it down. Like oppress the bastard. Now gimme your hand.'

Carol bumped her frightened hand at him without taking her eyes off the bonnet. She felt him grasp it and push the palm down onto the gear lever, his hand over hers, carrying the lever forward.

'Let this' — he tapped her left knee — 'gorgeous gam — up, very gently.'

The car started moving.

'Cigarette?' said Ben.

'I don't smoke. Ben, how do I stop it?'

'Wet your finger,' he replied sinking back down in the seat.

She licked her finger quickly. 'Like this?'

'Good. Now hold it in the air.'

She did. 'Like this?'

'A bit higher.'

'Like this then?'

'Yep. Now do you feel it getting drier?'

'In the wind. Yes it is — it feels dry.'

'Now. This is the hard bit. You mustn't move your finger at all or take your other hand off the wheel. This is the only drag about big American cars. Okay. Now you have to jump up and wet that finger again.'

'You're having me on.'

'Please yourself.'

'But Ben, I've never seen anyone going through all that to stop a car. It's ridiculous.'

'How many American cars have you been in?'

'What I can't understand is why you want me to do such a ridiculous thing.' Carol was staring rigidly ahead at the flying sands. 'It seems so primitive.'

'Anchors are primitive.'

'I meant you. Your tactics.'

'Forget it then,' he said, obviously not worried one way or the other. It was that that decided her, his disinterest in her decision; his disinterest in her. It was suddenly clear to her that her freedom lay in obeying his wishes; more, in discovering them and then obeying them. The bald man in the barber's.

'All right. I'll try,' she said. She clutched the wheel until the bones in her hand showed white, and tried to prepare herself for swift and sudden action. The wheel pulled her up inches short of her upheld finger, her tongue flicking out and in hopelessly before she plopped back into the seat. The car had altered course by about forty degrees and was now plunging straight towards the sea, headlights raking the creamy surf. Ben grabbed the wheel as the fender burst into the water and wrenched it right. The car slewed round in a great arc, a wall of water slapping against metal and mushrooming up like a depth-charge. They were gliding along the beach again before it fell.

Ben pulled the handbrake. They looked at each other. It was all right again. Carol started laughing.

'You are a bastard.' She was helpless with laughter. 'Why? Why?'

'I wanted to see your underwear,' he said flatly.

'You didn't?'

'No, your coat just covers it.'

'I meant, you didn't make me do all that jumping up and down just to see my underwear?'

'I wanted to see if you could lick your finger like that.'

'But why?'

'I guess I'm just interested in people.'

'You wanted to see if I was fool enough to try.'

'Please yourself, baby.'

'Although you knew that I didn't believe you.'

'Talker.'

They looked at each other some more, then Ben reached over and slid his hand under her hair onto the nape of her neck. His other hand flicked ash from his cigarette. Carol closed her eyes and her mouth parted for the kiss that didn't come. Ben caressed her neck languidly, almost inattentively, until she arched her throat like a purring cat. He watched her face in the light from the dashboard, her eyes trembling under the lids, her mouth silently murmuring as she leaned into his pressure.

'Get in the back seat.' His breath whispered hotly in her ear and she shuddered deliciously, pushing a shoulder up to protect herself.

'No, Ben. The beach. I can't—'

'The back seat,' and he flicked his tongue into the depths of her ear.

'Eee,' she said, making a lemon face. 'All right.'

Carol took his hand in both of hers and rubbed it against her cheek and then kissed the palm. She didn't take her eyes off him.

'Ben. Be gentle with me.' And then she said, 'My name is Carol. It's important to me that you know.'

His face came too close for her to see, a shadow looming and she felt a stinging pain on her neck and at once his tongue on the pain, molluscine, soothing.

'Charlie,' he whispered.

When she stood up her legs trembled and she would have fallen but for his steadying arm. She stumbled awkwardly as in a boat between the seats and onto the wide seat at the back, sitting in the middle and drawing her long legs up sideways onto the leather so that they looked longer. She began to shiver. She was excited and afraid.

Ben clicked open the door and got out. She heard his feet crunch on the sand somewhere behind the car but she couldn't seem to turn her head to look. Could he be nervous too? It seemed impossible. What was he doing? 'Ben,' she called. Her voice came out in little bumping breaths.

'Take off your coat. Make with the silken rustlings.'

She unbuttoned her coat and folded it over the back of the driver's seat. There was a briefcase beside her so she put that in the front too. Then she sat still again. Carol was wearing a brown and olive striped dress with a Victorian cameo at the neck: on her feet she wore brown flatties with a T-strap: her breath came in short pants despite the inclemency of the season. She looked like Alice waiting for the Rabbit.

As Ben got in he pushed the button and the hood rose over them, shutting out the sky.

'Oh Ben,' she said, as his arms closed around her. She felt her back suddenly naked under his hand: the band of her bra slackened and her breasts bore downwards in the lace; then the thick fabric of her dress felt in folds about her waist.

His hands brushed gently over her breasts, the nipples stiffening, following his slow palms, then springing back.

Carol made little snorting noises with her nose: a row of jolting f's: then s's as his teeth closed on her nipple. She became oblivious of the cold leather at her back, did not hear the little tearing noises as she moved her body. His hand filled her senses, pulling and squeezing, like a drowsy milkmaid at her breasts.

Ben knelt on the floor in front of her and rolled up her skirt, pushing her hands away as she tried to undo the suspenders; he bit her thumb and her hand jerked away. He ran the back of his hand across her belly, then along her thighs, then — first left, first right, and round the corner — up to her loins. He slipped a finger under pantie elastic and moved it along the damp hair.

Carol said, 'Aaah,' like a straining constipate, the vocal range being small and a certain overlapping of designation unavoidable.

Then, 'Oh God!'

Then, 'Touch me there.'

Then, 'Ben, Ben.'

She thrust her bottom off the seat in an ungainly movement to help him roll off her panties, prancing her legs in a panicky drum-majorette fashion to kick free of them. Ben's head was bent over her, his overcoat, caught by a corner on the door handle, spread out like a bat. His hands softly pushed her knees apart, and then his mouth was on her. 'Oh do it,' she said, but he let her plunge around contacting nothing while he did some very supporting feature stuff on her thighs. And then she felt the shock of his touch on her again and desperately jerked herself up and down, like a gnat-bitten horse against a post. One of her arms was thrust out straight pushing her hand flat against the cold glass of the window.

When at last she could open her eyes he had gone. She did not immediately realise where she was. She felt as if she had been ill, sick perhaps with some fever that had left her depleted and unclean. He had not made love to her, not given himself at all. Her body shook uncontrollably.

After a while the beach became a seaside resort, bereft now of the gay wrappers and broken glass of summer, and Ben drove smoothly between the tarpaulined chalets onto the slipway and rejoined the road. She sat in the back seat in the shadows. Neither spoke. When they reached the outskirts of town Ben asked where she lived. Then he said, 'You feel humiliated don't you?'

She swallowed hard. 'Why did you — do that?'

'Suggest reasons.'

'No Ben. I don't want to play that game.'

'You loved it.'

In the back seat she covered her face with her hands.

'Didn't you?'

'Please — I don't want to talk about it.'

'Disgusting. Unnatural.'

'Don't!' She shouted the word in sudden violence. 'Don't speak about it!,

'Unspeakable,' he said.

He drew up outside her house and she lunged at the door handle and almost flung herself out of the car, but he had her firmly by the wrist. He stared up at her from the driver's seat. She made no attempt to pull free, just stood there, head bent, a hand shielding her face from his gaze; hopelessly off balance and near to tears.

'Now dig this. I'm giving you a reason and it's the last I'm ever giving you. When I've told you this you're going to push the gate and run into the house and scrub yourself all over in the bathroom. And all the time you'll be thinking about this and when you make it into your little bed you're going to think about it some more. Tonight the wind blew you over. I don't need that kind of help.'

He released her arm and she saw that he had strapped his own watch to her wrist, the face down against her pulse. She stared at it, uncomprehending.

'Now you know what time it is,' he said. 'So ruminate, ruminant.

As she pushed against the cold iron of the gate, the huge car made for him a Wellesian exit.

10

When Ben unlocked the door of his room and turned on the light he saw a folded square of paper on the lino. He bent and picked it up. The message was written on exercise book paper and the writing was large and childish —
YOU ARE BEEN WACHED.

He stared at it for the length of a minute, unblinking, unmoving. The draught from the open door sent the dust drifts silently tumbling across the lino. His image was caught in the mirror on the wall. Ben from the side, his near arm pulled straight down by the weight of the briefcase, a curve of wrist growing out of his profiled chest, the logical arm engorged; he closed his eyes — he seemed to he waiting as a tower besieged seals itself off and waits. Then his fingers began to move: slowly, lovingly gathered the paper into a ball and crushed it until the whole body shuddered in the convulsion. When he opened his hand the paper was spotted with blood. It fell to the floor. He leaned back against the wall his face wrung, sickly.

He switched the light off and padded surely between the vague shapes of furniture, twitched the curtain aside, and looked out. He looked straight down on the streetlamp and through the blue brightness he could see the empty street. If there had been anyone in the street he would have seen them. They would have stood out like fairground targets against the blank of hoardings opposite. There was nowhere to hide. The house stood at the corner of an intersection, thronged with dock workers and fish bobbers at midnight and at dawn, a busy thoroughfare by day; now at 1am it was deserted. He could see the two empty crates below that the newspaper-seller sat on, and the old cigar box that held his change.

He stepped softly into the corridor. The whole house was asleep. Some pensioner refought Inkerman on the second floor with shrill, cracked oaths and then fell to mumbling. Ben stood outside the paper-seller's door and listened. Not a sound. He turned the knob in that slow spooky way that people exhume for night. Doubtless it looked worse from the inside, causation invisible, but the occupant was pounding his ear in incurious sleep. It was quite light in the room. He had not drawn the curtains because, wrapped around his trousered legs, they would not have made much difference. Leg not legs. He had one personal leg and one wooden leg that lay apart from the parent on the table. Beside it, flanked by a sauce bottle and a crumpled newspaper containing fish skin and a pair of impossible chips lay the exercise book. Ben leafed through the book finding nothing but block capital headlines. Mr Wilks took his work seriously and practiced headlines of pith and moment for his placard.

On the mantelpiece Mr Wilks kept his books, paperbacks stacked at one end, library books at the other, the yard between them asserting his honest intentions. All the books were about espionage except the library books: one of them was on counterespionage and the other on ciphers. Ben leafed through the book of ciphers until he found a strip of newspaper marking Mr Wilks's place, then he turned back two pages.

ELEMENTARY CIPHER 'D': NUMBER SUBSTITUTION.

Ben read the directions, then replaced the book. He crossed to the table, picked up the biro and drew two blue and perfect circles on his wrist above where his watch had been. Then he sat on the end of the bed and gently shook the sleeper awake. Mr Wilks reluctantly surfaced, massaged his eyeballs and pushed a sentry's face at the figure on his bed.

'Who is it? Who's there?' he demanded.

'Ben Herod, Mr Wilks.'

'Hold on a mo — let's have some er —' but Ben stayed his waving arm. 'We don't need the light. It's about the note.'

Mr Wilks's voice became hoarse in token of secrecy. He sat up in the bed and prefaced his reply with a long, deliberate wink.

'You got my message? Communiqué?'

'Indeed I did, Mr Wilks,' said Ben. 'Now what's it all about?'

Ben offered his cigarettes, lit two and handed one to Mr Wilks.

'You're being watched, Mr Herod.'

'What did he look like?'

'Short. Fat. Sixty-fiveish. He had an assumed voice.

'An assumed voice!'

'No two ways about it. It was assumed. Didn't fool me for a minute—'

'You're a pretty hard customer to fool, I'd say Mr Wilks.'

'He sounded like a Bosch but I could tell. It was assumed all right. I know Brother Bosch as well as I know you. I've heard them gabbling away over the sandbags more nights than I care to remember. "Handy hock, Fritz!" That's what we said to the POWs — prisoners of war, you know.'

'That was in the Great War? A rough show that one.'

'Rough! Rough wasn't in it!' Thus, the paper-seller asserted seniority. 'I lost my leg in that one.

'You gave your leg for your country? I'll warrant you'd have given your life too — eh, old man — if the call had come?' His back to the light, Ben nodded. It was not in question.

Mr Wilks nodded back. 'Oh yes, not a lad in our battalion but wouldn't have given all his limbs if the call had come. Or laid down his life.'

'Gladly.'

'I think we knew where our duty lay.'

'When did the call come for your leg?' Ben asked, then quickly added, 'How did you lose it?'

'Mons. I was I/C Donkeys at the time. I was a bit back from The Front at this old farmhouse. The Frogs had skipped of course.'

'Huh!'

'Trust them! So I'd taken over the barn for the donkeys, until they were needed. I'd just got the mail from Blighty and I was sitting on this crate reading. I'd just got comfy, boots off, feet up, and I was reading away as if I was at home by my mother's hearth — except the paper was a week old, of course. Well, where was I?'

'Sitting in a barn. The war hardly existed for you.'

'*Voomm!*' cried Mr Wilks, 'a ruddy great bang went off outside. I jumps up off the crate and has a peek and I sees that Jerry has dropped a 501 on the farmhouse. A direct hit. Only one wall left standing. The blast has blown the shutters off and all the shelves on the inside, but this is the funny part — one window was still in. Intact!'

Ben fingered his poll.

'Rum that,' he mused.

'Rum! You're telling me!' Mr Wilks cried, utilising his jubilant National Unreadiness voice. 'It was uncanny. I leaned on the door, chin in hand, and tried to figure it out. I forgot where I was. The war hardly existed for me. You get like that after a bit — hardened to it. Don't care. Then I remembered the donkeys in the back. I had to get them before Jerry had another crack at us.'

'You set your own life at naught,' Ben asked.

'I'd got past that. I just never thought about it; you don't after–'

'Do you think Jerry knew about the donkeys?'

'Hard, to say. He may have and then again he may not.'

'True.'

There was a long silence during which Mr Wilks remained with his mouth open in readiness should his thread become clear to him. Strain as he might he could not see beyond the black silhouette at the foot of the bed, the lamps beyond and the night sky.

'You feared the Bosch were zeroed on your manger?'

'That's only natural isn't it?' challenged Mr Wilks, irritated.

'Natural,' said Ben.

'I had to shift them right away before they had another go. They were all shoved in together — six of them, jammed — away in a manger. So I got their bridles and climbed over — it was a gate I'd tied to the front of the manger to keep them from scooting. They really had the jitters and that bang had set them off barging around against each other. Restive. Highly restive. So I started talking to them and stroking them to calm them down. I could hardly see them it was so dark. I was squashed up between them somehow and they kept on breathing hard — sort of "Huh Huh". I had this bridle in my hand and I was feeling for the right end when all of a sudden I got this terrible pain in my foot. Agonising. Just for a split second I thought it was one of those shooting pains that everybody gets, you know, but it…'

'I never get shooting pains,' said Ben. 'I've never met anyone who has ever had a shooting pain like that.'

Mr Wilks was openly contemptuous; he snapped into his Outraged Opinion voice — 'I've met thousands of people who are regular sufferers from shooting pains. Scores! You must be a bit peculiar. Search me why you're so special.'

'I hope you don't think I'm being rude, Mr Wilks, I certainly didn't mean to be. I just wasn't clear about the shooting pains and I thought it best to ask.' Ben extended his hand. Mr Wilks was magnanimous in victory, they shook hands heartily and Mr Wilks thought twice as much of his friend, legion of himself.

'It didn't pass off, though, it got worse and worse. Searing. I tried to bend down to have a look at it but I couldn't get room to move. I was jammed right up against those donkeys. I caught sight of the crate where I'd been reading and then I realised. My boots were still over there! One of those ruddy animals was standing on my foot!'

'You'd forgotten to put them on again. Seeing that window had put them clear out of your head,' cried Ben.

'Exactly. All I had on were my thick issue socks.'

'But you kept your head and tried to figure it out.'

'That's right! I tried to figure it out like you do when you're being driven mad with pain. Now, how can I distract this donkey's attention, I was thinking? So I started lashing out all round me. I pushed and I punched and I shoved and I barged. The thought of that shell lent strength to my arms. I thought I was a gonner. They wouldn't budge. Weighed a bally ton. I tried to figure out which one was on my foot. I suspected it was either Kaiser Bill or Wipers Willie.'

'What made you suspect them?'

'The Process of Elimination.'

'Phew,' said Ben, admiringly.

'Oh yes. I kept my head in spite of the searing agony. I remembered in some book I'd read — I was a great one for books, still am — about this camel driver who'd got out of a tight spot by twisting his mount's balls. Well, thinks I, if it works on camels, why not donkeys?'

'You had to be ruthless.'

'I'm not saying it was a thing to be proud of. You'd expect it of an Arab or a Dago or a Frog, of course, but it didn't feel natural to me. I suppose it was the pain. I've never felt pain like it nothing to touch it.'

'They say pain like that can be unbearable.'

'Unbearable's putting it mildly! Pain like that can make a man do funny things.'

'You were at the end of your tether.''

'I felt along his belly but I couldn't find them. Either my arm was too short or I'd picked Nelly Dean in the dark. Anyway…' The young Mr Wilks and the old Mr Wilks merged into the same impasse: the story went no further for either. The speaker fell silent again.

'What did you do next?'

'Eh?'

'What did you do next? You said you could hear the creak of harness and the canteens chiming together and you panting in the dark with the pain.'

'That's right,' said Mr Wilks. Perhaps, after all, it did go on. 'I remember I could hear the canteens bashing against each other — like bells they were — those cowbells they tie on cows in the Alps.'

'I've never been to the Alps, I'm afraid.'

'No, I haven't either, come to think of it. That's what they sounded like though — perhaps I've heard them on the radio or somewhere.'

'That's right!' Ben snapped his fingers. 'They were on a request programme last Thursday. A most distinctive sound.'

'Ah, that would be it then. Of course.'

'And you were —?'

'At the end of my tether. Nearly passing out, blackness, a long black tunnel opened. Yawned.' Mr Wilks could not go on.

'You made a last despairing —'

'Flailed about, punching and pushing —'

'Set your teeth.'

'Despairingly I set my teeth into the nearest donkey's nose. I held on like grim death. Not a sound — just these distinctive bangings and creakings.'

'Shied away leaving your foot free.'

'I dunno,' said Mr Wilks morosely, exhausted now, just wanting to get the leg off and be done with it. 'I passed out then. When I came to the lads had got me out somehow. I never had time to ask because we attacked that same evening and took Jerry by surprise. They left me behind — my foot was a mess — the arch was broken. I couldn't walk. I wore this big white plimsoll to keep the wet out, but it was no good. When they got me to the field hospital it was too late. Gangrene. They took the leg off and shipped me home. And that was that.'

Reflection was at a premium for several minutes, then Ben said: 'War is Hell, Mr Wilks. It takes our young men from us and sends them back crippled.'

'It's all wrong,' said Mr Wilks, bitterly brushing ash from his shirt-front.

Ben moved up the bed until he was a foot away from the paper-seller, stared at him levelly for several seconds and then at length nodded in satisfaction. 'You'll do, Mr Wilks. British, resourceful, discreet, plucky.' He rested a hand briefly on the Wilks shoulder and leaned forward. 'You know, Mr Wilks, today we're still fighting for the same values. The same cause in which you gave your lower leg. Now I don't have to tell you who we're fighting or why —'

'Communism. Democracy.' The tenderpad of the freedom-loving nations rang loudly in the sleeping house.

'Hush, man,' hushed Ben and rose to peer both ways up the corridor before rejoining his companion. 'Yes, I can see you've done your homework. I don't have to dot the i's or cross the t's for you about the cold war and espionage and all that. *You* know. That's why you've been chosen. I can't tell you who you'll be working for, but I can say that Her Majesty's Government will not be shall we say ungrateful.'

Mr Wilks brandished his winking eye, thrust his tongue into unshaven cheek and prodded his elbow into Ben's ribs: the point was fairly taken. And even as he sheathed these signals, Mr Wilks unfocused into an oak-panelled study of approximately ten foot by twelve. The speaker, tall, straight, still a fine figure, stood absently toasting his seat at the fire through parted tails. His clipped hair and moustache re-echoed the expensive gleam of cutlery, candelabra, crossed assegais on the wall. The only man for the job, almost a boy really, languidly lounged in the deep leather chair and swirled his firelit port in a crystal goblet. It was, of course, a pose. His red Saxon ears missed nothing, noted every nuance, inflection in Intelligence's voice.

'I'm going under cover for a bit. They've got onto this address. God knows where the leak is but we're working on that now. You see, in this game a word here, a nod there and the whole thing is shot to hell. Of course, I don't have to tell you that — you know how to keep your eyes open and your mouth shut. You are ideal-ly placed to keep observation on this house, who comes to visit, who comes asking for me — anything at all that strikes you as suspicious. And remember! They may come disguised as police-men or vicars or even sporting assumed voices — whatever it is, I want to know. Which brings me to this.' Intelligence took a large, plain manila envelope out of an official-looking briefcase, and the young subaltern caught sight of the two blue circles on his wrist. His very blue eyes momentarily came to life with sardonic amusement.

'Lost your watch?'

Their eyes meet, locked, British eye to British eye fairly matched in mutual divination, before Intelligence conceded the ghost of a twinkle.

'Now listen carefully — in here you'll find your story. Memorise it then destroy it — eat it, burn it, but get rid of it. Stick to that story through thick and thin if you're questioned. Understood? Good.' Intelligence rose and placed the envelope with deceptive casualness under a sculling trophy which often did duty as a rinsed shrimp-paste pot for collar studs and barely franked stamps. 'If they do question you, show a bit of difficulty remembering. Let it come out bit by bit.'

'The old realism,' interjected the slim young subaltern, 'Blazer' Wilks to his cronies in the Ninth.

'Exactly.' Just the flicker of respect in that bronzed, leonine face and it was back to business. 'In this smaller envelope you'll find a locker key with a numbered disc attached to it. It opens locker 14 at the railway station. Not the lockers by the entrance but those over by the Loo. Now I want you to inspect that locker tomorrow afternoon. There may be nothing there and there may be a suitcase. If there is a suitcase, I want you to take it down to the old pier and sink it. Make sure it goes down. Go out to the end where it's deep. No-one is to see you or follow you. Got it? Good man. If I want to contact you further I shall leave a note in the suit-case. Now we'd better use a code. Let me think. Do you know the Elementary Cipher "D": Number Substitution?'

'I do.' There was nothing languid in the crisp reply.

Intelligence vouchsafed a hint of amazement.

'The deuce you do! Good man. Now, number six: expenses. Here's a fiver for now — more if you need it. Don't look like that, man — we don't expect you to risk your life for nothing! I know you don't expect reward for doing your duty but this is a little beyond that. You know the official joke — patriotism is not enough?'

'I've heard that somewhere,' frowned Mr Wilks.

'Can we count on you?'

'You can count on me, sir.'

A great deal of manly feeling went tacitly into that handshake.

'Still favour the right pin I see,' said the voice that kept Mr Wilks from his sleep. The agent had gone but he couldn't seem to relax and he could feel his body trembling with excitement under the curtain.

'Silly thing really,' the drawling young voice said. 'Crocked it on a Bosch ranker's throat in the hand-to-hand at Mons.'

And the voices fell silent at last. Mr Wilks had one more thing to do. Pushing back the curtain, he worked himself painfully off the mattress and stood, one hand against the wall for balance. His flannel shirt hung to his knees and below, his single leg shone pallid in the moonlight. He looked like a banner. He seated himself at the table and inspected the wooden leg. It was the National Health model, the Speedlite Special with the hinged stride action. The rubber tip was worn thin. With a fishknife he prised it off, replacing it with a new instantfix tip from a box in the drawer. Then he oiled the hinge.

11

The door opened on John and her eager, nervous smile faded. 'Power cut?' said John, wryly according himself full Turd Status with clasp and ribbons. 'I'm sorry it's only me. I'm always sorry its only me.' He closed the door. 'Drab dependable John, tweedy poke agog with goodies for urchins and mangy dogs. Can I come in?'

'You are in,' said Carol and sat in her scarlet rocking chair in a despondent slouch. She was wearing her very big deal dress and gnawing a fingernail. John noticed that she was now wearing a man's wristwatch.

'Expecting someone?' A comment rather than a question.

'What makes you say that?' Her voice was formal, embattled; she didn't look at him.

'Man-wise he opined the laird at least from the fluttering embonpoint of her...'

'Oh for God's sake, shut up!' She flung a furious glance at him to establish his range and her voice rose to assault him.

'What business is it of yours? I don't want you making everything cheap with your stupid comments. If you've got something to say, say it and get out!'

In the silence that followed this outburst John grasped the doorknob and waited for hurt pride and dignity to sweep him headlong through the door. Nothing happened. Spontaneous reactions, he reflected, were what he notably lacked: if you were waiting for the quick to be stung or even a good bridle, it was best to bring a packed lunch. He held his breath and watched, as he had known he would watch, the gap between them silently widening, the congealing of possibilities. Every detail of the scene lay separately and graphically on his retina as in, already, memory; dark hair falling, eyelids squeezed shut, the whitening tendons of the hand on the red wings of the chair; the chair held at the extremity of its backward flight. He could not close the door behind him on that arrested movement, tension pent unreleased, releasing like a joyful breath on his departure. A moment to stay the hand of the beadiest suicide.

Then he spoke: '*Oh Carrie, Carrie. In your rocking chair by your window dreaming, shall you long alone. In your rocking chair by the window shall you dream such happiness as you may never feel.*'

Carol began to cry.

He knelt before her and she crumpled toward him. But the chair swooped forward at last and their heads clopped together in painful cerebro-cannon. John had to cork his ouch and dared not stop stroking and patting the heaving shoulders to touch the aching lump over his eye. She must have felt it! He felt a twinge of annoyance at her single-mindedness. Why couldn't he cry like this, drowning in it, sloshing about in it, undistractably distraught? How bloody lucky she was to have these special orifices to evacuate grief; he only got things in his.

'I'm so sorry, John,' she sobbed. 'I was being a bitch.'

'No, no, no — of course not — not at all,' and he used the conversation as a cover because the mechanics, the commonplace grunts and fulcrums of lifting her to her feet must not disturb her remorse. Over her head he scanned the bookshelves for the books he had lent her, but they were too far off and presented only a fence of penguin orange with a wobbly white band. She had probably left them in some bee-loud arbour. Carol lifted her face from his damp shirt front, the second she had wet for him in a week. Her mascara, lonely cosmetic, had blotched around her eyes like a silent screen vamp's.

'John, why did you say that about dreaming by my window?'

'I just said it.'

'You must have meant something.'

'I suppose I intended it rather as a sort of compassionate revelation of the depths of ordinary men and women in all their frailty and humanity with the compassionate scalpel of the artist. That really.'

'It was very beautiful,' she said reverently. She patted his chest in a sort of attaboy gesture and went to clean up. John watched her walk into the kitchen. The line of her panties beneath her dress rose and fell rhythmically like seagull's wings against the cumulus of her buttocks. Thought John, this is the life, sitting in her chair, head nobly sculpted against the cold morning light.

'I like your dress,' he shouted above the splashing tap.

'Do you?'

'You look like a china Dresden doll. In your pretty skinny frock.'

Carol emerged looking shiny and scrubbed. She pinched the fabric of the skirt and held it away from her the better to appreciate it. She frowned: 'You don't think it's a bit too…?'

'Emphatically not. If it were a fraction shorter the whole effect would be frankly frivolous. And of course you score heavily with the backs of your knees.'

Carol turned away from him to look down over her shoulder at her back view. She threw her weight on one hip, then the other.

'Yes, but John, don't you think perhaps it's a bit…?'

'Daring? I should think not! It hints at contours beneath but that's all right. Hinting is okay. And it doesn't hint more in one place than another — ideal for a first date, you know. Well, I'm keen on Ornette Coleman and Jean-Luc Godard and Axel Oxenstierna and I have a nice body in general. That sort of dress. Like selling you've got lots of interests. No-one could take umbrage at that — even Our Lord said "This is my body", and nobody thought He was being over-salty. Now a heavily localised hint is a very different matter. If you drew those street signs — you know the pointing hand on a cuff — This Way, Up Here — on your dress all converging on your parts like a magnetic field and tried to pass it off as Pop or Op you'd get run in. Well, the point I'm making here is — Christ where did I put it — yes, that would be too daring.'

'You know I wonder about you, John. Sometimes I really think you're crackers.'

'Oh yes,' he said, remembering, 'I took your books back. The librarian was very stroppy with me.'

Carol came over to him and smiling felt his brow. Her fingers faintly smelled of some pampering soapbrand.

'Do you write that old tripe in exams?'

'Only the names are changed.'

'And do you pass?'

'You're joking! Of course I pass. I'm the only truly literate person I know.'

Carol went and got a hairbrush and began to reduce her hair to order. She stood in the mathematical centre of the room tilting her head this way and that as she brushed. John did not tie himself to the mast, but he watched enthralled. Then she stopped and folded her hands together in front of her. John noticed that there was no visual distractions within yards of her slim, solitary figure; it had to be confession time.

'John,' she said. 'I think I'm in love.'

John looked at the hairbrush in her still hands. He thought it resembled a dead centipede, back down, myriad legs aloft. 'And aren't you happy?' he asked.

'Frightened,' she said.

Sits, he thought. Squire closeted, snickers in dusty lust. Carol sat on the edge of the bed.

'Frightened that it won't work?' he asked.

'Frightened because I can't recognise myself in it. I didn't know that I was capable of this sort of feeling. It's…' She broke off to stare into space. 'It's as if I were born anew — born with no outer skin so that —'

'Sloughed it off,' John suggested.

'Yes.' Her whole face implored his understanding. He did some nodding. 'Can you understand that, John?'

'Intellectually.'

'But you've never had this feeling yourself?'

'No,' said the giant brain on a trolley, sci-fi hit of the '60s. She twiddled the brush. 'How can I explain it? It's like a new colour. One that no-one had ever imagined before — a colour as pure as red or blue but without a name.'

'And you can't relate to it?'

'It blinds me, John. I lose myself in it. There's no me left to relate.'

'Hmm,' said John. He was beginning to feel the strain. The whole conversation was like trying to sew a button on a fart. What had happened to the bloke in all this sloughing and colouring? John knew that she could wax post-coital over Grannie Smiths, so he probed for the catalyst.

'Does this colour come to you strongest with the lights out?' He retreated quickly. 'I mean with your eyes closed?'

Carol covered her face with her hands. 'You've got me all confused. Colours. No, not colours — that was just an example. I was trying to make you understand the feeling.'

John's overloaded brain tipped into inhibition. 'Perhaps he's coloured? The man?' he said, then wildly, 'I mean — is he English, this chap. Does he love you…?'

'You think it's funny!'

'No, no! Does he love you is what I — it's not funny — I want you to be happy —' he jumped up to prove it — 'I'm not making fun, taking the — I'm not jealous — I didn't hope — Oh I know I'm a failure —' he flurried on horribly conscious that he had introduced the fustian theme of their relationship which had obviously not occurred to her. He seized her hands and the hairbrush. 'Carol, I know I have no claim on you, we're still friends aren't we? Look, just say the word and I'll go — you say. I'll do whatever you want. I can't go smaller than that or I'll disappear.'

Carol clicked into place. She patted his head, changing it to a ruffle between equals as she realised her omission.

'Don't let's talk about it any more,' she said with a sad smile.

'Change the subject,' said John.

'Yes.'

'Can I have my books back?'

'Oh yes. They're on the shelf.'

Poor John, she thought. The very last person in the world to be telling about her love. How could she be so tactless? She looked at his familiar bulk, his large red hands slowly preoccupied among the bookshelves, the back of his neck shaggily intent and unmoving. Oh God, how much simpler it would all be if she could love him and not this strange frightening — Ben. Did she love Ben? Was it love? In the car, that… No name. It was all confused. Did she feel what she felt for him or for herself, her own body awakening? Narcissus in thrall to the silvered fishlimbs spreading… She might never see him again. The thought was pain to her.

'I want you to take me to the seaside,' she said suddenly.

John's hand retrieving stopped in the air, body turning in the slow series of amaze.

'It's winter,' he said, recalling his wide ranging oaths of abnegation even as he spoke. 'Well, March.'

'Nevertheless,' she said in a final manner.

Eyebrows haughty, she drew chinky sticks at eyelids' end with a tiny paint brush.

So they went to the seaside. Laden with sixteen books in two carrier bags he ran heavily after her to the railway station, eyes intent as a lepidopterist's on the fluttering rim beneath the thin blue dress.

'But Carol,' he said in the empty compartment.

'Read your books,' was all that she would say. John gave up and began sorting through the books. He remembered lending her *Sister Carrie*; it wasn't among the pile in his lap. She certainly hadn't read that. He thought of all his lovely books, of all the ones she must have lost on buses, on trains, in cloakrooms, woods and beaches; all the wonderful lives he had lived now roaring up and down the country, set at naught by nose-pickers, sold by the yard to dealers,freighted, thrust up bottoms in God knows what barbarian emergency: lost.

'Where's my *Sister Carrie* then?' His eyes were accusing.

Carol only smiled at the sliding grey landscape through the window, her face, as in her thoughts, imposed between her contemplation and its subject.

On the pier the wind was biting. John removed his US issue combat jacket and put it around her shoulders. Then he flailed at himself in ostentatious martyrdom, but she refused to notice.

'Look at the waves!' she cried and tripped down the stone steps. Behind her back he stabbed the air viciously with two fingers but the gesture got snarled up amid the painful string of the carrier. He was glad to huddle in the shelter of a breakwater, the bags splayed out beside him like the udders of a floating cow. He presented a blank profile to the cold flinty pebbles and grey seas. She was off somewhere enjoying some attic bloody muse while he froze. What did she care if he did freeze, dropped dead, pined to death for his books? Rhetorical — strictly rhetorical. A robot was all she wanted, an obedient robot programmed to buzz encouragement to her hermaphroditic drivellings; to dissipate his voltage glowing empathetically at the mouldy waves. Right! He was a robot. He tried to get a tell-tale twitch going in his jaw, but it was sunk with all hands in the general chattering of his teeth.

'John. Help me down please.' Carol wobbled along the slimy edge of the breakwater, her shoes dangling from her hand, arms outflung. His khaki jacket was much too big for her, hung vacantly from her shoulders, the epaulets like handles on her upper arm. Her whole demeanour begged his protection, offered her frailty to him to cherish, him Tarzan, me Jane. He glared at the wet splash marks on his jacket and clanked towards her, arms whirring into position. Carol concentrated on his strong grip about her waist, the warm red hands making a delicious cocktail with the wet contact of the pebbles on her bare soles. Half a mile from this spot she knew the car had come to its momentous halt. She tilted her face up for his kiss.

'Got a pain?' said John, sitting down again between his bags. Carol opened her eyes again.

'How can you be so petty? What is the matter with you? You've done nothing but mope all afternoon — I don't know why you came.'

John was just ready for this.

'I'm being petty because I am petty. I thought you were ape about natural unaffected behaviour. Next, nothing's the matter with me except that I'm cold unto death because you have my nice warm jacket and my fingers are all strangled from the string handles of these bags. Should be more painful, ought to be painfuller still only you lost at least half my books including one hard-back. Next, I have not merely moped. I have shivered and I have reflected. To take a random example — why you should want me to kiss you when you can see I'm still the same humdrum pink I was before you met this psychedelic colour dispenser. Last, I don't know why I came either.'

'Good job you're such a masochist,' said Carol laughing down at him.

'Blessed is the lamb,' he replied, cross-legged and slowly bowing to indicate the lasting and worthwhile in a world of hectic kicks. Carol sat beside him and peered into his face.

'John — I want to hear the truth. Do you really worry about all those things — your books and so on?'

'Yes I do. I gnaw my mind down to the cuticle about all those trivial little things. Ashtrays was the worst Now it's traffic.'

'Go on, then.'

'Ashtrays?'

'Yes.' Carol rested her chin on her fists in the standard listening position and thought about something else. The beach was so different by day. Sad. Like the shards and embers after bonfire night? Not very good. The exact place must be under the sea. It was on sand and this was pebbles.

'Ashtrays caused me to give up smoking,' John arrestingly began. 'I was a twenty-a-day man and a feared Boss Recidivist.

Air was too thin for fulfilling breathing — I could take it or leave it alone. Have you read *The Confessions of Zeno*?'

Carol nodded, wheels and flesh squealing in her head.

'I hadn't got what it took to be a real smoker. I lacked the hell-raising quality of the real smoker. I worried all the time. I used about a hundred IQ units worrying about the ashtray. You see, it takes vast organisational skill to deploy an ashtray in a drawing-room so that you can flick without fear and read without distraction. You know your rocking chair? The hardest spot on earth to smoke in. You have to estimate motion, wind, slipstream and trajectory every time you tap your ash. It's like taking lighthousemen off in bad weather. Joseph's got it. He's the one real natural I know. He just never thinks about it. He scribbled one out on my knee in the pictures once…'

'I never knew you were so neurotic John. I couldn't be like that. It seems like such a waste of time.' Thus Carol doused the monologue.

'What else would I be doing?' said John.

It started to rain, the wind sloshing it down on them in squalls. John sprang up and stared wildly about him for shelter. Behind him ran low lumpy cliffs, homely as Flanders in the dissolving rain. A hundred yards away he saw a changing-hut.'

'Come on!' he shouted, clattering over the pebbles, a bag in each hand. A string handle pulled out of its limp wet socket and he scooped the splitting bag to his chest and ran on. When he reached the chained and padlocked door he jittered up and down in panic.

'You'll have to break the window,' said Carol.

John thought that was just typical. Didn't she realise that action submerged the self? Attracted the police, too.

'How do I do that then?'

'Punch it in or something — we've got to get in!'

He skipped up to the window and pushed at it with the sound bag. 'Blast. They're only paperbacks. See — if you'd only returned my hardb…'

He stood at attention, eyes accusing under streaming fringe.

'Use a stone you fool — be quick!'

'Too much noise.'

'Oh God.'

'Burglars put treacle and brown paper over the pane and then it pushes out quietly in a lump,' John said.

'Really?' said Carol sarcastically. 'Now if you get out of the way and let me do it.'

'Oh,' said John. 'Right.' He thrust the two sodden bags into her arms and took a headlong running dive at the door. There was a rending crash as John and the door disappeared inside, the padlock and chain whirling after them like a bolas.

'Are you all right?' Carol tumbled books onto his heaving chest as she bent over his prostrate form.

'Did it make much noise?'

In the gloom she was laughing. her mirth disproportionate, wide mouth rushing at him noisily as if he were a meal. He lay still, watching her almost in fear of such excess. When she had finished she helped him into a sitting posture and began weakly butting his shoulder with her head, and laughing over-tired laughs as he had seen putty-necked three-year-olds do.

'Finished?' he asked icily.

'Oh John, don't be cross.' Another butt awarded. 'It was just so — so spectacular. No-one heard you — there's no-one around for miles.' She pushed herself up using his multiple bruising as a launching pad and stood looking at the rain through the splintered door-frame. She could smell the damp and the dust in the hut and felt somehow reassured. It was all so familiar, so right. The dim light from the shuttered window fluttered softly on her eyelids as she moved. Like a stick clattering along the railings of childhood, she thought, and remembered her notebook. She felt happier than she had done for a long time; then she remembered Ben. And all of her happiness, the clean cold wind, the rain outside their refuge, John himself, suddenly felt stale and confined. She would never write from a life of such contentments when the life itself was already pale nostalgia. And oh God, must Ben be the answer?

As she turned away from the window to John, John said, 'A sea monster!'

Carol saw that he was holding up a large baggy rubber object. It had been lying in the corner.

'Let me see it.' She stretched out her hands,

'Wait till I blow it up for you.'

John sat cross-legged on the floor and inserted the nozzle in his mouth and started to blow. Knobs and carbuncles began to erupt from the flabby rubber, lines and circles of colour stretching into place until she saw that he had conjured up a silly seaside dragon. 'I feel like,' he panted, fingers pinching the valve, 'one of those fat cherubs at the top of maps.'

'Blow some more!' Carol cried.

He blew some more features into the monster. His temples throbbed with this act of creation, and he barely heard Carol announce that she and it were going for a swim. Opening his eyes at last, he found himself frankly facing a dark pubic forest. His face burned. He fumbled for light words to cover his perturbation, but the swollen monster, finding its valve unguarded, rushed windily out of its rubber prison and his urbanities were swept aside by racking coughs. By the time the fit had passed the startlingly mature emblem, the quarry of his Vilest Thoughts, had disappeared from view. His moist eyes darted about over the top of the diminished monster; his mouth by association or by chance, sought the nipple.

'Hurry up, John. Haven't you finished yet?' Standing on one foot with her back toward him, Carol glanced at the cowering shape behind the swelling dorsals. She was pleasantly aware of his scrutiny: she hugged herself appreciatively and smiled at him. 'You come in too — you're wet anyway.' She snatched the squeaking monster from him and was gone, bottom beautifully jouncing, quick-footed over the pebbles to the sea.

He could see her larking around in the shallows. The sea monster bobbed up and down and made blundering rushes against her legs. He could appreciate its motivation, thinking, oh to feel the grip of those strong thighs along one's flanks, that brisk hair-crackle on rubber back. He stole a glance at her scattered underwear on the floor. There was the lace border that made the ridge, a brief moment ago cloaking the mysterious forest. She had hidden nothing from him because she was only a woman and now he knew everything and everything was spoiled. In a little while he got up and started to undress.

'You look like the Bile Beans Girl,' he said, shivering at the water's edge and rummaging fluff from his navel.

'Get in! Get in!' Carol shouted. She slid off the monster's broad back to dissolve in pink fragments against the breakers. He stood watching the heaving seas and brooded upon his nudity as rain pelted on his head and shoulders. He wished he could be innocent. A buoyant bubbling Carol threw water into his face, seized his hands and dragged him into the waves. The cold made him frantic and his stumbling feet caught on a subterranean rock;

sinking, he flailed at the waves and his flung hands struck her breasts, the sea monster, a flotsam fish — he never knew which. When he surfaced he saw Carol riding the bucking steed against the crazily tilting horizon, one arm raised above her ragged hair. He swam towards her. The water was thick with seaweed that had torn away from the rocks, and he wriggled in revulsion as the cold fat rinds caught in his fingers. Plunging on through the waves with his powerful crawl he reduced the distance between them to a yard, but strain as he would the yard remained. He raised his head and stared across the rain-pocked surface at the laughing, gleeful rider.

'I can't can't catch you!' he shouted.

Carol paddled the monster round in a circle towards him.

'Now try,' she said, and as his fingers touched the squealing wet sides of the sea monster, he knew that he too had been caught.

Running blindly along the pier in the rain Carol cried because of what she had done. She would have given anything to undo her crime, to have the last ten minutes back again in which not to do it. His frightened face crumbled into a terrible anguish and her fingers had jerked away from his flesh. She had used him as she would an object, lugging him onto her with the sympathy of an irascible removals man, chafing boy scout-wise at his cold limp sex to kindle a performance that was over before she knew it had begun. She had proved to him that he was, as he had always said, admitting anything, really quite dead.

The wind plastered her wet dress against her running body. The station jerked up before her, offered nothing but flight. Let him forget her, forget her. She saw him curled into a whimpering ball on the floor of the hut, his arms hiding his face from her shocked pity. If he ever found out that it was on this beach she had... The garden shed of her childhood swam nauseously before her eyes. Only at the station did she remember that her panties lay among the ruins of his pride in the beach hut, but purity of association spared her the significance of their juxtaposition amid the rubber and chains.

Ben waited for her in her room. Ben had it made.

Part Three

1

On Thursday Dr Ostbahn knew suddenly, in the act of forking a strip of bacon into his mouth, that his obsession had entered a new phase. He had no tangible proof of this, yet he knew that somehow, though his relationship with Ben had returned to its outer form of silence, overnight, even as be fitfully slept, the gears had been slipped and the serrated edges of his fear locked in the new position.

As the knowledge struck him he dropped the fork onto the tablecloth and experienced a minor heart spasm. Mrs Ostbahn fumbled the cotton wool from the bottle and fed him two of his little white pills. 'You can't go in today dear. You must go and lie down and take it easy.' She stroked his hand, skin against skin, for solace: the Ostbahn beneath was untouchable, adamant. He donned the disreputable overcoat, the bread-line hat and, groping for the spectacles in the pocket, breasted the icy winds of the city. Mrs Ostbahn watched him through the net curtains and when he was out of sight she cried because only a man in love with a young, passionate mistress acted as he had been acting.

The doctor did not go to his surgery, had not been there for two days, since his declaration — syndicated — of independence. Instead he walked to Ben's residence and took up his customary position opposite, standing foresquare to the house with a giant hoarding at the back of him like a mount. He wanted to be seen by his tormentor, seen as he saw himself — Nemesis — a daily and punctual rebuke; Ben would be forced to come crawling out of the house and negotiate before he, Ostbahn, told all. He had forgotten to remove his disguise. He stared fixedly at the windows, willing the curtains to twitch.

A few people walked past him on their way to a late clock-in, or an early shopping, who knows. Going somewhere. The newspaper man opposite watched him watching Ben's window. Time passed. A man poked threepence at the doctor and asked for the *Mail*. He stared at him wildly and the man went away: nothing made sense.

Two youths bounced past. 'Heard that Ostbahn yet?'

'That's bleedin' old stuff now. Course I have.'

'You're all mouth.'

'Who's all mouth?'

'You. Mouthy.'

The doctor's name hung in the air long after they had disappeared. The doctor no longer knew if his name had been spoken or, never absent, hung in the air of the city for pointing fingers: everything was possible. Violins rose in his chest and tears pricked his eyes behind his glasses. Couldn't Herod see that he was an old man? He was no use to him — he was finished. He pushed the glasses up off his nose, failed to notice the thick bundle of delivered papers under his arm, and wiped his eyes on blunt glove-ends.

He slumped, frozen, into his leather surgery chair, and between his gloved hands emitted a harsh, shuddering breath. Yes, he would go to the police. He would give himself up. No more chances, no more waiting. At once. Now. He lifted his head. His troubled eye fell on the telephone. Surely it had been moved. For twenty years he had kept his phone at a precise and oblique angle to the desk pad so that he could jot his messages without moving his body. It had been moved an inch or more out of true. It couldn't have been the receptionist because...

Madness suddenly tilted at him as he saw it. In each concavity of the receiver, upside down and secured in place by strips of adhesive tape, hung an egg. The egg in the earpiece said, in licked indelible pencil: *Ladies. Bring Your Eggs To Ostbahn*. The egg in the mouthpiece, similarly wrought, said: *Ostbahn Goes To Work On An Egg*.

The doctor's hand shot out and seized the receiver from the hook, releasing an empty, insect droning as he held it like an

overturned jar of wasps. He stood up abruptly. He panted. He
licked his lips.

He smiled. 'Now!' he said.

'Now,' he said.

'Now,' he said.

'Now,' he said. He laughed. He pulled open the drawer and felt
for a knife. He cut the flex an inch from the receiver. He held it aloft
and twisted it this way and that. He laughed at it. It was evidence.

He snatched up his briefcase and undid the straps. He laid the
receiver very carefully on top of his instruments. He put the newspapers inside and he smoothed them. He closed the briefcase. He
wrote in big letters on his pad: *Not Ostbahn*. He wrote it again on
his desk. He wrote it again on the wall. It was biggest on the wall.

He knew it was behind him in the street but he just went faster.
Nothing could stop him now. His coat spread out behind him.
Once he stumbled and nearly fell. His glasses were shaken free
from his nose and fell onto the pavement, but he didn't stop. It
was close behind him now. At the corner he flung his head to the
side to look. The street was a narrowing tube between walls; he
could see right down it. Framed by the shoulders of two women
and projecting above them like the sight on a rifle he could see
him. He lifted the briefcase and shook it. 'Now !' he shouted. The
figure didn't move.

The market place in front of the police station was filling up
again and he plunged into waves of advancing and receding
sound. People were everywhere in his path and he had to push.
Bubbles of sound burst in his face with a bang and a rush of air.
Soon he was treading the bubbles under his feet; they squeaked
and tickled him and that made him giggle. His legs were bubbles
now, now his arms. He let go of the briefcase. He could feel the air
hissing into his chest, getting fuller, growing bigger, lighter, no
weight at all; he *was* a balloon. He laughed as he felt his feet leave
the ground, falling, falling upward, above them all, in the sky,
above the noise. Two faint moons came towards him and the
nearer they came the more indistinct they became. Bigger and
bigger and he was swallowed up in them.

Ben pushed through the crowd around the fallen man. 'Stand
back please. I'm a doctor,' he shouted, doctor-like behind
Ostbahn's glasses. He knelt beside him among the split fruit and
curly wood-shavings on the concrete, undid the collar and
slipped the tie down to get at his heart.

'My briefcase.' He lifted his head from the trembling chest to jerk a direction at a policeman. 'Over there.'

'Funny,' thought the policeman, hoarding a rich jest for the canteen. 'It's got nought nought on it. Licensed to kill. Very reassuring. Ho ho ho.' His finger rapped against his helmet. 'Here you are sir.' He forced a wider circle around the pair. Heads waved like anemones to get a better view; most of the stallholders, realising they could not undercut this, brought their sandwiches over and made a lunchbreak of it. Ben opened the briefcase and peered in. It was hard to see what was inside through Ostbahn's glasses but he saw enough to flop the lid over his rummaging hand.

'It's all right constable. This man is a patient of mine. He's had a heart attack.'

'I'll phone for an ambulance, sir.'

'If you would.'

His hand came out of the briefcase holding a hypodermic syringe. He held it up to the light and saw that it was half full of some yellowish liquid. The crowd held its breath. He pushed the plunger, shooting a yellow stripe onto the concrete and then wiped the needle on his handkerchief. *Ooh-Aah* said the crowd as at fireworks, and watched the needle dimple then puncture the flesh at the neck, and deposit its killing air bubble into Dr Ostbahn's carotid artery.

When the evening edition hit the pavements Otto Ostbahn finally made it to the number one spot, not for his disc, or even for his laudable moral recovery; typically, he made it on his passivity; he had lain still under a hundred eyes while a killer slid two inches of hollow steel into him and let the daylight through.

The city police snapped into action. They were always thorough and this time maniacally thorough; the newspaper had given the jesting policeman celebrity coverage after all, he had handed the killer his weapon. Within the hour they had Ben's description to a T. Height — average; build — average; eyes — blue; brown; black; glittery cat green; hair — yes; clothing — dark, average. Better, they had the killer's glasses — unusual and distinctive glasses, thick lenses in steel frames. By systematic investigation they were able to trace them to Dr Ostbahn. They did not find the briefcase and they did not find Ben. Both had disappeared long before the ambulance drove into the square to carry the dying, banderilla'd old balloon to the irrelevance of modern medicine.

2

At seven o'clock sharp Mr Wilks was at his pitch clad in his usual overcoat and beret, a thick khaki scarf wound about his neck against the cold. He felt ready for anything, despite a sleepless night. He had chosen his fastest shoe, a light construction of canvas and rubber and his wooden leg moved more easily for the oiling. If the action came thick and fast — well, he was the boyo.

Meanwhile, his mind on cut and thrust, he sorted his papers into handy ranks and made caches of various combinations of change. He spent a long time on his bulletins, worried for the first time that they did not look sufficiently genuine, sufficiently the work of a pukka paper-seller. Because today he wasn't. Today the whole set-up was a front. No good if passers-by rumbled him at once. He rubbed his fingertips in newsprint and smeared a bit of black around his mouth; newspapermen did lick their thumbs for riffling, he remembered. It would all be a sight more convincing if he had a kiosk, perhaps a big yellow one like the Frogs had.

He felt better after he had sold the first paper of the day. A bloke on a bike had bought the *Mirror* and cycled away without penetrating the disguise. Mr Wilks did a big turnover in *Mirrors* up to nine and then *Times* and *Telegraphs* after that. That was the pattern of things. No good getting aerated about it like that canvasser last week. Tall studenty geezer with a tatty beard had bought the *Morning Star* at midday, right out of phase of course. An argument had developed about the pattern of things in the paper-seller business but Mr Wilks had argued him flat: workers till nine, then the uppers. Natural Law.

Throughout the morning no-one penetrated Mr Wilks's ensemble. By midday he'd sold most of the national dailies, had a cup of tea and was waiting for the early edition of the local paper. The street was flowing as usual, bits of conversation, averted accidents, the flash of traffic; all there for anyone with a taste for fragments. There was even a bonus today in the shape of rival electioneering vans, both equipped with loudspeakers, each discharging broadsides of raspberries and slogans as they passed on the road. A procession marched down the road, banners flying, everybody out of step but nevertheless calling out the time: Left! Left! Left! Sloppy bunch. Mr Wilks shook his head contemptuously and spat on the pavement when he saw that self-same scruff-arse student at the head of the marchers shouting the odds and blowing on a whistle.

He watched the passing show with half an eye. Foremost in his mind was the Mission: he was thinking ahead. To the locker. To the wharf. Bombs like bowls fizzed in his thoughts. He cut the string on the evening bundle, waving absently to the van driver, placed the papers on his box beside a careful handful of change, and set off for the station.

He hadn't seen, had not had occasion to see, the inside of the railway station in fifty years, so that he stood in the entrance arch almost like a released lifer, conscious of eyes on him too, incredulously eyeing this incredibly altered prospect. The smoke had all gone and with it the memory of a foundry from which he had been flung, remade, passed over, hobbling on crutches on a raw, new, dead leg. Well, that was all a long time ago and leaves had grown on that leg. Fate, he reflected, was bringing him full circle. His country had called again and here he was, ready to embark.

He walked warily across the station parallel to the platforms, past the porters, past WH Smith's kiosk, the vendomat complex, up to the stack of key lockers. All right so far. No-one was watching him. Pretty muzak, released by aerosol into the atmosphere, was distinctly reassuring. Whistling along with the tune, he braced himself against the wall of tin lockers and felt for the key that Ben had given him.

Number 14 held, as promised, one small cheap fibre suitcase. He took it out. What he did next was capable of swelling his chest a year later, though his motive was no clearer. What he did was to spread the morning paper on the floor of the locker, lock the door and poke the key through the slot grille in the door. The key fell with a muffled sound onto the newspaper inside. He had executed it perfectly: it could be, perhaps, a sort of trade-mark — sang-froid with a flick-of-the-wrist. That would show 'em!

He bought a pennyworth of privacy in the subterranean Gents to satisfy his curiosity about the contents of the suitcase. Inside, he found a tape-recording and a Chalimeff set — moustache, goatee, eyebrows and a little tube of glue, all attached to the display card. On the card was written in Elementary Cipher 'D' the words *Well Done*.

After reading the walls and door he left the closet and marched, canned Sousa at his back, out of the station to complete Stage Two of his Mission.

The open car cruised slowly along keeping pace with Mr Wilks as he dot and carried breathlessly down the road. A fresh-faced young man in a sheepskin coat with a pretty rosette, prize bloodstock, stood up and, leaning his elbows on the windshield, looked carefully in every direction. It was all clear. The street, an unpopulated line of warehouses and scrap-metal yards, Mr Wilks the sole pot-walloper in view. A bit of ragging would be quite in order. He lifted the megaphone to his curly lips: 'Sir, would you sin against Nature? No, of course you wouldn't. Would you repudiate the aristocratic principle of Nature, the eternal principle of force and energy, for mere numerical mass and its dead, dreary weight? No, of course you wouldn't.'

The driver and the girl with leaflets began to laugh. Nigel had a bloody good sense of humour. Bloody funny.

'Sir, would you deny the individual worth of the human per-sonality? Raze — with a Z, sir — the very foundations of human existence and human civilisation? You don't look like that sort of a chap to me, sir. Monstrous do you say? Indeed it is. But that is what the Socialists are asking you to do.'

Mr Wilks hurried faster, looking rigidly to the front. The last thing he wanted was to be followed, picked out in a spotlight of noise and attention. Not today, thank you. His ancient heart thumped painfully against his ribs.

'We've all heard them. Smash your Monarchy — smash your Church — smash your Public Schools. There's nothing they wouldn't drag in the mud. Are they worthy to belong to a great people? What do you say, sir? They call themselves Intellectuals. I don't know what that means. You don't know what that means. But we both know that Intellectuals make a Bish of things.' The candidate shifted his position to include the occupants of the car more fully in the joke. He stood up very straight and held one finger horizontally under his nose. His voice became raucous and bawling. 'We healthy people instinctively close our ranks against these Intellectuals and they run this way and that like hens in a poultry yard. That's Instinct not Argument. We are a Great People — God-willed and Blood conditioned. Our collective egoism is sacred. Are we going to tolerate these polluters of Blood, these deniers of Race?'

'No!' and 'Certainly not!' chorused from the car. The girl sang out: 'Hurrah for Smithy!' and then gave a nervous laugh.

'The socialist is the ferment of decomposition in a People! He is a pygmy who imagines he can stop with a few phrases the gigantic renewal of our People's Life. Shopkeepers and pacifists — they are insignificant little people, submissive as dogs and they sweat with embarrassment when you talk to them!'

He raised his clenched fist in the air like a hammer. His voice grated metallically through the megaphone. 'The long-haired socialist youth lies in wait for hours on end satanically glaring at our clean white Womanhood. He plans to adulterate her Blood with repulsive crooked legged black bastards! Who brought the blacks here? The ruckspawn scum, swarm of the jungles brought here to bastardise our Race? The socialists! They are paralysing our Will to fight!' Flecks of spittle hung from his chin but he made no move to wipe them away.

'Don't overdo it, Nigel,' said the driver, exchanging anxious glances with the girl. The candidate was overdoing it a bit. One had to be a bit more circumspect about things nowadays. Of course, it had been a long hard grind and the candidate had not stinted himself, sleeping in hotels, eating at cafes, talking with anyone. No doubt that awful Bell type had taken his toll on the candidate's patience. They were rather relieved when Mr Wilks turned off into a sidestreet leading to the wharves, the way blocked to traffic by erect sunken cannons.

'Set your souls aflame!' screamed the candidate to blank

walls. Frightened, the girl stood up and tugged at his coat. Above his upheld fist the sky streamed black with wheeling gulls. He would not be moved. 'A torrent of fire bursts forth as from a furnace and a Will of Steel is forged! A people hard as iron! When they cast in our teeth our intolerance we proudly acknowledge it. Ours is the Standard that dispenses with all others. One Will must dominate! One Discipline must weld Us together! As the magnet attracts steel splinters, so does Our Party attract the Strong, the Pure, the Unpolluted! It is my unalterable Will...'

The car disappeared from view bearing the upright candidate into oblivion.

Mr Wilks looked down into the dirty water at the rising bubbles of Dr Ostbahn's vocal remains. He heaved a great sigh of relief.

3

She started off with love but it became something inde-
finable. She could see that his was a tortured flame and that
attracted her. She could always feel his eyes on her wherev-
er she moved in the flat; he needed her. Not a courtier's eyes but
the eyes almost of a guard. In those first days, hers reflected only
the racing sky and the clouds. His need fleshed her slim legs and
added pounds to her breasts and buttocks so that she saw herself
as hills, as an oak tree, as the earth, about which his lightning
played and spent itself, her sward his sheath. She remained at
eight stone two, but she thought big. This was the love as therapy
stage and it lasted two days.

In the mornings he searched the newspapers and she cooked
his food. She didn't trouble him at all, initiated nothing, accepted
everything and let the remaining bubbles of her independence
surface and dissolve. Whatever trouble he was in she felt loom-
ingly as something of blood and honour like a Theban tragedy,
but she never asked him about it.

Ben finished eating his breakfast, wiped his mouth and said:
'Why do you always speak between inverted commas?'

She smiled at him, ready to play.

'I don't understand I quote too much?'

'Think about it.' He just sat and waited.

'You mean that I always speak secondhand sentences from
books?' Carol put her elbows on the table and searched his face
for encouragement, showing with her smile her readiness to

admit other viewpoints and any stones he cared to throw. 'Well, it seems to me that books are relevant to me, to my situation. The truly great writers will always be relevant in every age. Human —um—human nature is unchanging and this is what the novelist portrays. The novel is a distillation of wisdom and observation…' She found it hard to go on. It was difficult to know how much he knew; whether this wasn't insultingly basic.

'Or perhaps you mean — yes, like John, that one is restricted by physical confines. Your commas of course. That one's Self is trapped within the confines of one's body. Kafka and so on. I'll quote for you — "Love has pitched his palace in the place of excrement" —something like that. I don't think that. That sort of thing seems to me a sickness. It's very sterile you know, books where the hero is always squeezing boils and glaring at his hands. Well, did you mean that sort of thing?'

'I'm just putting the coin in,' he said and laughed when she jumped up.

She wanted to slap his silly triumphant face but instead she began clattering the dirty plates together.

'Playing God are you?' she acidly said and scraped a shrill knife at the rinds and tomato skins. She had turned half away from him and didn't know he had moved until she felt his body suddenly up tight against her back. She tried to push him away but he had her wrists imprisoned, her palms flat on the greasy plates, her body pushed forward over the table. It began as a rape; she would never have chosen the moment or the position. It initiated the end of the love as therapy phase and the beginning of the more complicated phase. The real change occurred as he forced his way, slick now from the proper channels, past the prissy knot of the sphincter and into irredeemable impropriety.

From now on it seemed to her that he stopped the sun in its tracks and ruptured the full-bellied moon, her motor, enthroning in their place the gravitational tyranny of the bed. Her room became a prison and her body kept her there, hooked by a tab of thin cartilage like a hung garment, to the edge of some mortal, vertiginous free-fall. She burned with shame and she continued to feed the flames.

'Ben?' she said timidly, conscious of repetition, 'could we go out —just for a walk?'

'What's with you?' he said.

'I feel so stale stuck indoors all day. I need some fresh air.'

'Me, I like trusty old air best.' He looked away from her and yawned, stretching his arms above his head like a broken catapult. The morning editions lay around his chair in a disorderly heap. He wore only his socks and a new wristwatch, identical in every chromium detail to the one he had given Carol. 'So open a window,' he said at last.

Carol stared listlessly out of the window. She scratched at the back of her hand and then examined the marks.

Ben looked at his watch. 'Bedtime already !' he said in a surprised tone. 'Get your clothes off.' He got up and switched on the light. It was midday.

Carol could never get him to set foot outside the house while it was light, but he didn't actually prevent her from going out. One afternoon she set off for a walk in the park but she had to return within half an hour because she was exhausted and frightened. Everybody she passed had seemed unreal, alien; not alien as John had seemed, but actually physically alien as if they were made of something else. Then it occurred to her that it was she who had become alien, cutting herself off from them by her depravity. Only her room behind drawn curtains offered her sanctuary. Only there, with Ben, was her secret safe.

'Visual agnosia baby,' said Ben. 'Very sterile, like squeezing boils or glaring at your hands.'

After that she confined her journeys to the supermarket up the road which stayed open till late, filling her undyed hessian bag with polythene wrapped from the refrigerated interior. At 11pm Ben turned his attention to the night and took that apart.

'Go get the car,' he said, tossing her the keys.

He had taught her to drive the huge convertible, not well but well enough to drive it from the all-night parking lot to the house, stopping to get the tank filled on the way. Outside the house she had to toot once on the horn and then move over quickly for the swift silent shadow that hit the driver's seat and wrenched the car from the kerb in one blurred movement. He always drove very fast and very carelessly and it seemed to her that he was indestructible. There was never much conversation. Going out for Ben meant swapping a stationary box for a moving one.

'This do you?' he would ask, jerking his head at barely discernible fields.

'No, let's go on a bit.' She could say that and he would drive on patiently until she saw what she wanted. He was not so much considerate as interested in the ritual. Apart from her freedom to choose, her choice meant nothing in itself because the entire countryside looked the same in the dark. They both knew that. This was her hour of exercise. When she had chosen, he would pull the car back off the road and turn off the lights.

'Okay. See you soon. Be good.'

The door would open and she would feel his kiss chill on her cheek in the night air as her feet moved over frosted unseen furrows. Carol loved this hour of silence and solitude and she hoarded it throughout the day, his day that fed on hers, as abjection hoards the promise of sleep. This was her hour. In this hour she could call the shots as capriciously as she wanted because it was the sole exercise of her franchise, the last of herself. The world was simplified into two equal bands of darkness, the lower one on which she walked black and invisible, and above it, separated by a horizontal line that was really the curve of a circle too vast to imagine, stretched the faintly paler vault of the sky. Sometimes she walked towards an objective, the black pole of a tree, a steeple, and sometimes she just walked until her watch told her she had come halfway. In this hour she tried to make her mind a blank, to purge her mind of him and just exist. She never obtained relief however, because Ben, the Ben that she loved, presented no separate identity. The heaviest burden of him was in her senses: he was her.

At exactly the half-hour, turning back, she would see a tiny red light explode silently in the darkness, a point without depth or context, illuminating nothing yet drawing her in faith ever nearer to it like a sleepwalker. When she reached the car Ben would stare at her for a long moment and then as completely return to the obsession of endlessly unrolling tarmac. Carol, at this furthest point from her freedom, knew that without this hour she would leave him. And he must have known it. He never mocked at it or turned it into a game. It was his only defeat.

Every night they would cover three hundred miles, returning always before dawn when she would drop him at the house and return the car to the parking lot. As she walked back to the house, her blood seemed to drone in her veins and her eyes had the rigid, neutral quality of headlights. It became an unvarying routine each night, every road, merging in memory into one. Only once did he stop the car, abruptly, shockingly, and she felt his hands seize her shoulders.

'Shall we stay here?' His eyes bored into hers.

She was stunned. She didn't know if this was one of his painful jokes and she didn't know how to reply. The windscreen wipers hissed over the wet stone-coloured glass. They were a mile from some anonymous market town, three counties from where they had begun.

'I don't know what you want me to say.'

He didn't reply. She could feel a terrifying rigid tension in him, willing her to speak but she could not understand what he wanted from her.

'You know I'll do whatever you want Ben.'

When he spoke she knew that she had failed him, his voice hard and casual because of her equivocation.

'I wanted you to make your choice. It was up for grabs.'

He turned away.

'But why here?'

'Because it's elsewhere is why.'

'Yes but so is everywhere — everywhere we aren't living now.' She tried to make a game of it and then in desperation made to touch his shoulder.

'Ha ha laughs aplenty,' he said swinging the car round in the road and keeping the needle at eighty all the way home.

And all the next day he drowned her every word with a furious static of crude and unfunny jokes, introducing each one with a nudge in the ribs and a yelped 'Have you heard this one then?' Carol bore his revenge stoically, ironed his shirts, cooked his dinner and tried to initiate burgeoning and bright topics of conversation. By mid-afternoon she was exhausted. She felt as if she had just spent a week trying to direct a very colour-conscious Nigerian through labyrinthine suburbs to an impossibly pronounced destination. She went into the bathroom to escape the grinding fun.

She leaned over the communal sink and stared at her face in the mirror. She looked terrible. In just a few days her wistful melancholy, the asset that had set the boys waving their hats, had become a poverty of all expression, leaden, inanimate. Love didn't agree with her. In the webbed glass her face looked yellow, shining faintly with the greasy patina of sleeplessness. The area around her eyes appeared bruised. Resting the heels of her hands on the cold porcelain sink, she leaned forward until her nose touched the glass, and watched herself cry. But not depraved?

Surely she didn't look depraved? Could she have experienced all this, the sore, wracking obscenities that her body forced her to, and yet not show it on her face?

And yet look no more damned than an insomniac.

John's words came into her head, a handful among so many empty, amusing torrents, spoken she remembered, in her room, now hers no longer and scoured of all former association as one scours an instrument of surgery. 'Snapping green eyes are your portion.' But now she cried.

Ben stood beside the open drawer of her writing desk, a sheaf of paper in his hand.

'Did you write this?' he demanded, tapping it with the back of his hand. 'This cleave and yearn jazz?'

She nodded, incapable of defending herself.

Without haste or anger he tore the paper across, tearing it again and again until it lay in a random mosaic on the floor. Then he stood still to watch what she would do. Carol felt nothing. It seemed inevitable, right, the action suited to the hands. She was him: she said nothing.

'Nobody sucks me like an orange. That crap sells me short, baby. Short by a million miles. I'm bigger than you know. So don't try to trap me with your shit scribblings.'

Carol stood very quietly and looked at him. He was cracking up. It was suddenly very clear to her that Ben was a man falling from a great height, conscious only of his damnation and resolved that his death should shatter the earth. She knew too that her silence had won her a great victory.

'Get on the bed,' he shouted. 'And leave the door open.'

'No, Ben. You can do what you like to me but not with the door open.

They stared at each other across the length of the room. It was the first time she had opposed him in anything.

Carol lying on the unmade bed, a blanket loose over her legs. Pushing back her hair because it irritated on her hot skin. 'I can't sleep. I can't just go to sleep like you do. Perhaps it's the light.' She lifted a flaccid arm to shield her eyes from the 5pm light bulb.

'Poor little baby,' he said. He placed his thumbs very gently on her eyelids and gently stroked the quivering skin.

'My eyes have been hurting me,' she said in a little girl voice.

'Poor eyes,' Ben said, 'so tired, so sore. Ben stroke them.' He increased the pressure of his thumbs, denting her darkness until a spectrum of dazzling colours burst into splinters behind her eyes.

'Make me a new colour, Ben,' she murmured, lying there still and acquiescent for his magic.'

'I will if you tell me a secret.'

'I don't know any secrets. I can make one up if you like.'

'I don't want you to make one up. I want you to tell me the secret about you and John.'

'That's a sad secret. You don't want to hear that.'

'What happened that day when I moved in with you baby. That's what I want to hear.'

'There's a bee under my eyelid. Did you know that? It's a bit of a quote.' Carol was very near to sleep now. 'The bee is a secret.'

'Colours baby — do you see them? Pretty colours, beautiful colours for my baby's eyes. All the jewels and rainbows and catherine wheels in the world for my baby to play with. I'm making a new colour for you baby — it's coming true. I can turn the world for you. I can revolve galaxies under your eyelids.' He buried his mouth in her hair. Carol drowsily took his hand in hers and kissed it. He sat up carefully so as not to disturb her.

'Ben will give you something to help you.' He took a key from his suit in the wardrobe and unlocked his briefcase. He took out a syringe and held it up to the light. It was still empty from the last patient, an emergency job in the market place. In the kitchen he collected a glass of water and a spoon, then he carefully tipped a little white powder out of a bottle in the briefcase.

'I'm nearly asleep now darling,' Carol murmured, her voice already blurred.

Ben sat beside her on the bed and placed his hand on the curve of her hip. He had hidden the key to the briefcase where even frantic fingers would not find it. He held the loaded spike in his free hand.

'This stuff is the greatest for dreams,' he said, smiling kindly. 'Strong on new colours too they tell me. Now that little secret bee may give you a little sting, but that won't worry my baby.'

'How much will you do for it?' he asked, his eyes on the streaming road.

Carol clutched his arm and said: 'Anything you want. You say.' It wasn't really bad yet but she could feel something blindly stirring in her dark.

'You know something baby? You've really come out of your shell since I've known you. You're a really switched on Sixties Romantic now.

'I want it!' Her voice came out loud, surprising the little bit of her that was still capable of a mild thing like surprise.

'I don't think you should be too reliant on it,' he said and pursed up his mouth in a considering gesture. He slowed the care. 'This looks like a nice spot for a walk. What do you say?'

'Yes, all right. I don't care — anywhere.'

'No no.' He pushed his solicitude at her like a curled whip. 'I want you to get the best out of it. Suck it dry baby. Don't want to waste it. I keep you in all day so you just take your time about choosing.'

'This will do!' Carol was already opening the door. 'I don't care I tell you!'

She was gone only ten minutes, stumbling over the sharp mounds in the dark and cutting her knees and hands. She could not find the car again. She became hysterical when she couldn't see the bright red parking light and she started screaming. When at last she found it the doors were locked. Ben was invisible behind the steamy windows and she couldn't make him hear. Perhaps he had left her! Sobbing she fell to her knees in the road, her splayed fingers rushing shrilly down the cold wet glass.

'I'll do anything. I'll tell you the secret. I'll tell you!'

'You know best, dad,' Ben said into the receiver. 'You know the market — it's your turf.' He leaned back, craning his neck to look up the spiralling staircase. All the doors were shut. 'You name it — she'll do it. Yep, take my word.' He listened again and then said, 'I need the bread.'

A long pause. He frowned and began to wind the flex around his wrist. Under his jacket he held a gun gripped between his arm and his side.

'I said so, didn't I? And bring the money, see. Yes, she can cop she's got great big eyes for it. Yeah, she's wearing me out. Yeah, beatnik number–skinny–long hair–very cute. She could be crazy.'

Finally, Ben repeated the address and rang off.

Later, Carol moaned as he moved inside her, levering her senses free. Sweat stood along her hairline and in the creases of her throat.

'I'm going to make you a big star,' he whispered.

4

John stood on deep carpeting and watched a horny Ruritanian princeling tear his ticket across, then hold the door open unceremoniously with mauve and gold-piped buttocks. Gorgeous stars looked down from gilt frames. Their breasts bore signatures artistic and personal like dropped string.

The usherette carved a bright path down the incline for his squeaking boots; he excused himself along the knees and sat down. His posture, because of his height, was that of a cellist. Knees splayed to each side and wedged under the ashtrays, perforce annexing sixpenn'orth of Lebensraum to east and to west. He tussled bonily for the arm-rests. The western neighbour appeased an inch at a time before John's inexorable advance and finally gave up, blotting a false cough to save face. The eastern neighbour dug in and held. Elbow waggled against elbow in the strain of deadlock. John switched his tactics to an attack on the eastern satellites. He fired a strategic toe up the arse of the man in front, coaxing him from grave to acute: east slumped more easterly to see: John captured the arm-rest.

Master, he retracted the back of his neck and tilted his face up to the warmth of the screen. In the cinema, and only there, he was a lion for his rights. Of the countless backdrops presented to him at birth only the cinema delighted; only there did he, veteran spectator, feel at home.

His fingers idly began peeling tiny torpedo rolls from his ticket. It was the adverts. He knew them by heart, anticipating each, yearning slightly ahead of the scheduled hunger, thirst and acquisitiveness. He bought nothing when the lights went up for intermission. He hated the lights. The audience sat revealed, horrible, pasty, screwing their faces backwards to stare at each other. Yobs bobbed down to the saleslady, whistling. John sat still and faced forward, correct and orthodox, and waited for the main feature.

It was from this screen just three weeks ago that he had learned of his father's death. It had appeared in fizzly writing on the film itself, a completely unbilled guest appearance.

WILL MR JENKINS PLEASE CALL AT THE MANAGER'S
OFFICE IMMEDIATELY.

He wondered now if the message had been erased, or was it perhaps even now travelling world circuits in *The Left-Handed Gun*, plucking a thousand Pakistani Jenkins's from their seats in converted Nissen huts to dip pressed palms in the manager's office and break out their whites. Blenching black Kwame Jenkins's storm the Exit pushbar to munch deceased parts for strength and virility, sadly overriding owners protests. Cahier critics hail subtitle as pure alienation, a triumph of style. 'Ah, the common humanity of it all,' he mused.

Bowelly architecture tastefully faded into a push-button twilight. The main feature began.

It was a British film with lots of heart, cautious French wobbles, and stolen freeze shots. John had hardly been out of the house for days so he tried to enjoy it. He concentrated like mad on the story, the acting, and the camera-work, but the Exit sign, the clock and the black cut-out bonse of the satellite in front offered strong competition. He tried spotting sources, his lips curling in the faintest sfumato of a sneer. It was hopeless. It was crap. He was not taken out of himself, but thrown back on his own thoughts. They were crap too.

Was he a pervert? Running nude into carwash tunnels to be flipped with chamois, prinked pink by rotating brushes, armpits gargled with needle-spray? Not like that perhaps.

Worse.

People around and behind sighed at him as he vacated his seat, stooped in consideration for the Less Fortunate, wending a simian way to the Exit.

It had been raining. He remembered how Carol had once been depressed at missing a manifestation of the elements. Well, not quite that. They had emerged, he, Carol and Joseph, from the cinema into bright sunlight to find the pavements drying.

'So what,' said Joseph. 'Rain ain't much to watch.'

'When you've seen one raindrop you've seen them all,' he said, amplifying Joseph, geeing them both up.

'That's not what I meant,' she said. 'It makes me think of time lost — really lost — not assimilated into life. All this has happened and we didn't know.'

'We've made it irrelevant,' he had offered but there were no takers.

'You don't understand,' said Carol, and walked ahead.

Now John walked aimlessly down this same street listening to the voices from summer and laughter from the past and he wondered why he didn't give a damn. He had lost her at the seaside. Fat man sez I have lost my little willie. He stands in the sea. The wind is blowing up the channel today. It's great when you're in! Hair-trigger showdown: watch it sister or I'll drench ya knees!

He had come home from the seaside, self-destruction on his mind. Naturally not a new departure; rather, a new emphasis. He had always favoured a passive death, a spontaneous incombustion under the wet green sticks of his empty existence. Now he saw sharp edges and violent concussions. Walking, he saw himself stretched like a starfish on the window-ledge, a watery sun refracting his pyjamas into a striped nimbus. The wind toyed with his rip-cord. He nerved himself to jump. Off! In the air remembering that he had not left a note. Then changing it, kicking out, legs churning a bedroom slipper from his foot, employing the running-in-the-air method vindicated by Jesse Owens, the Black Auxiliary of the 1936 Berlin Olympics, which won him the gold medal and set the Fuhrer gnashing among the Axminsters. And it carried him safely over the paving stones and into the rhubarb, his father's pride, tooth-roughening weed, jolting ankle-deep in stiff manure. Feeling how? Probably silly. Mr Plume weeding, straightening, not wanting to pry, great excitement on his face. Larf it off somehow. How? Morning. Reading Hedda Gabler. Overbalanced.

Have to go through his house — no front door key — to complete deadly purpose. Striped suicide ponders note in bedroom.

Imbalance Of Mind Disturbed. Very good. Ho Ho. Puts it. Pleased and proud. Not dead though.

John had taken to his bed for three days on a protracted blush-bat. That was at first, when death had seemed a serious proposition for a pervert. Then he had got up and dressed, putting on an old overcoat of his father's from the heap in his bedroom. His father had been some inches smaller but the coat went on. The cap, on the other hand, was enormous, like a great check table on his head. That was when he got the idea to try life at five foot five. Seen from his father's height, the house was a palace of material comforts; everything was to hand, spacious. And to five foot five six foot two was an affront, a haughty malcontent presenting nostril linings to every remark.

He had taken seventy pounds out of the insurance windfall and put it in his inside pocket, and as a final disguise before leaving the house he slipped on his sunglasses. He was lucky to get a taxi and he kept it waiting while he went into the gram. shop and bought, cash down, a gramophone and ten LPs. At the grocers he passed twenty pound notes over the counter with the request to keep food coming to number 23. He was safely home within thirty minutes.

He kept the disguise on, threatening the stitches in the overcoat with his exertions. Out went the TV and the radio, the chairs and the sideboard, splintering the door jamb and scratching the wallpaper. They made an impossible bottleneck in the hall. He did not dare go into the backyard because Mrs Plume was dawdling about with her washing, obviously crazy for chat. His impetus had slackened and he sat panting in the only chair, the one chair necessary for his new life, that was left in the front room. The sounds of a revolution shook the windows. The new gramophone was turned up beyond the numbers, playing the new music of Cecil Taylor. He had listened and the tears had rolled out from the sunglasses and down his cheeks.

The street lamps came on, blinking at first and then steady. John started whistling *Round Midnight* but his timing was way off and his timbre monotonous. His crooked shadow jerked ahead, a metronome. The really depressing thing was that he no longer cared about any of it. Everything passes, happens outside, is like everything else. And that's a cliché.

He saw the gates of the railway sidings ahead of him. There was no-one in the watchman's hut because there was no reason to watch the few dozen empty goods wagons quietly rusting into their rails. The real depot had been moved in the war and the railings melted down for shells. Not that that would have stopped them from hiring a man to watch the hut.

He crossed the tracks. The unnoticed downpour had washed oil and rust whorls into the puddles for some Carol to find and frame. He walked on and came to the jetty. It was nearly too dark to see the water but he could hear it slapping about like obese lovers. He walked past the dim upright of the flag-mast and out along the wooden catwalk. He knew now that his feet had been carrying him to this precise spot for the past half-hour, two miles on magnetism.

He rested his hands on the cold damp railing.

This was the last thing that his father had seen, image caught, water, sky, frozen flat final and unremarked on the retina as the hood descended. Had it spun, water rearing over sky, uncorrectable for ever as he fell to his death?

What a meaningless album these snatched photos would make, wrenched in spasm, eyes break, on sections of darkening wall, on cupboard doors, on gravel. And yet meaningful in that his last picture was perfectly meaningless like his life. Lives are lived out of context. What epitaph could he offer his father?

On an impulse he climbed over the rail and hung, feeling for the iron scaffolding below. His foot hit a strut and he carefully lowered himself until he was standing underneath the jetty on a wet, encrusted horizontal. The wind or the current must have drawn the fishing line backwards under the jetty until it had snagged on a cluster of mussels. It was too dark to see anything and he grew afraid of the immense presence of the sea. His body had sunk in this sea, his head filling with water like a cave.

What epitaph?

He swung back up onto the jetty and turned his back on the sea. The goods trucks stood black and heavy against the skyline. A noise to his left caught his attention. The halyard had blown loose and swung in the wind, slapping against the mast like a whip. John walked quickly along the rickety catwalk and, seizing the line, tied it in a series of figure of eights to the cleat.

'Very moving,' he said aloud, and then, feeling in his breast pocket for a handkerchief, discovered Carol's panties.

5

Joseph went straight round to the alley at the back of John's house in assertion of their special relationship. When John's father, that miserable old sod, had been alive he had had to knock on the front door like any tradesman. Joseph's friendly visits carried his unique stamp; ideally, friends never knew he was in the house until the bedroom door opened to reveal the hatted figure bearing a tray of tea, which he would share as he sat on the end of the bed. This was a very friendly visit. He had just read about Ostbahn.

It was difficult to identify John's house from the back because each house was alike, the same sale curtains, the same tamped earth gardens. A small reflex of protest at standardisation flicked through his mind, but it wasn't really his thing. The alley was full of cinder heaps, derelict prams, tIn cans and wedges of lino. Joseph crunched to the end of the alley and then, more slowly, back again. He looked over the wire fences for clues. Then he found it. The slob hadn't put his dustbin out. The lid sat above the bin on a two foot dais of rubbish.

Joseph pushed open the gate, doing the usual with his cigarettes and tugging the brim of his hat down over one eye. He peered in through the kitchen window and gasped.

John was walking to and fro in the kitchen, stark naked save for a huge check cap, and staring at the contents of the shelves. His behind was thrust out like a mandrill's and his knees were bent. He looked as if he were carrying the white man's burden, perhaps in his cap. Joseph's gasps clouded the window and he wilted slowly down the pane, seeking clarity beneath each puff, until he too stood unconsciously crouched, the counterpart of a pederast's book-ends. John waddled to the door and looked up at the hanging coats, then he stretched up slowly to touch the hook. There was wonderment on John's face. Joseph's nose was on the sill, eyes transfixed by the happenings before him.

John disappeared into the dining-room. No longer afraid to make a movement, Joseph rubbed the window clear and studied the kitchen. It was a normal kitchen, the selfsame kitchen of former visits. Dishes filled the sink and overflowed uphill onto the draining-board. Reassuring household names stood foursquare on the cardboard packets lining the shelves. So what was so fascinating? Why such big eyes for this scene all of a sudden? Joseph shook his head and tutted.

There was a wooden coalbox against the wall under the dining-room window so, as before, he had to present buttocks to watch the show. The same craziness obtained. John, gouty sleepwalker, peering up at pictures, china ducks and pelmets as if looking up an angel's skirt; his lips moved in secret wonderment. The room had been stripped of all its furniture except for one chair. A new gramophone stood in the centre of the room.

'What is it? What is it?' panted Joseph, as beside himself as a doppelgänger. His jaw had dropped into the nest of his rolling button-down. His hat brim was pushed up flat against the glass and his nose was slightly on the Kildare side. He looked like a fool.

John looked up at the light.

'You're having a vision! Taking a trip!'

John again raised his arm.

'It's a wasp! You're tracking a wasp!'

But the arm came down, touched nothing.

Joseph took a flyer. 'Neo-Nazi freak-out!'

John sat down in the one chair, crossed his hairy legs and picked up the *Radio Times*. Joseph couldn't see what his eyes were doing, reading or rolling, because of the wide peak of the cap.

'God,' said Joseph, his hand itching to cross himself, his principles keeping it in his pocket. Everybody was crazy! That fat pro in the knocking shop, the entire Ostbahn deal, John and the oven and now this. Another paid-up, card-carrying nutcase! He couldn't just go in and visit him now as if nothing had happened. He might turn violent like they did and he didn't fancy trying to hold his tongue and get a clothes-line round him. What a helluva note! It must have been his father's death that did it. What was it he'd heard about cerebral balance? Yes, when you'd over-loaded the brain, it just gave up and you started doing the exact opposite. That was it of course. He'd always walked tall and looked down his snoot at people; now it had struck — *Zocko!* — and there he was playing the flipside, creeping around all balled up.

Joseph took a last look at the sad ruin of his friend. There he sat, unnaturally quiet really, not a stitch on, reading the *Radio Times*. Good-bye old buddy. He thought he ought to go and tell Carol rather than blow the whistle on him, so he set off for her place at a trot.

In Carol's hall-mirror he shot his cuffs, put lick on his eye-brows and shot his trouser-bottoms from the niche in the back of his boots. His teeth arced like a Verey light across the dingy mirror. Then he galloped up the stairs. He didn't knock on her door, paying her the compliment of assuming her round-the-clock chastity. At her kinkiest, she would be sniffing some flower. He opened the door on a Colt .45. It was aimed at him.

'Hey hey,' he squeaked, 'don't point that thing at me — Ben! It's me — Joseph.'

The gun remained trained on his head and he saw with horror that the hammer was already back.

'You should of knocked, professor,' said Ben. He released the hammer, holding it against the spring with his thumb, slowly let-ting the firing pin snick to rest on the cartridge. Only then did he lower the gun to his side.

Joseph fell into the nearest chair. He tried to get his cigarettes out but his hands were shaking too much. Ben took them from him, lit four, kept one himself and put three between Joseph's unprotesting lips.

'Grandma, what big eyes you've got,' said Ben. The small sweaty figure rolled about in the chair and finally managed to stand up. The small sweaty face was very pale and very angry, so it shouted. 'That's a stupid bastard trick! What if that fucking gun had gone off! Eh! You'd have felt bleeding silly then wouldn't you! Pointing guns at people —'

When Joseph had finished emitting these cries and put the roses back in his cheeks, Ben extended a finger and tapped his chest. 'Why did you run out on me, fink,' he said.

Joseph went cold.

'What do you mean ran out on you? I've been out a lot is all. Can't I even go out without asking your permission?' His tone had a whining edge to it, but an edge nonetheless. 'I left you my number didn't I? You could have left a message. You never gave me your address. I don't like my room.'

'You chickened,' said Ben.

'I never,' said Joseph. He was scared to take his eyes off Ben because he was suddenly sure that he had been the mystery man who killed Ostbahn. If he'd killed once he could easily do it again. He had a gun to prove it too. Joseph thought that his only chance lay in posing as the rube he had been so effortlessly in the surgery. One bad hand.

'How's the old— er —second chance. Swell idea that,' he said. Ben sat on the end of the table and idly dangled his legs. He didn't look much like a killer in his square's drip-dry shirt and waistcoat. He wasn't even growing a moustache. Joseph wondered how he had ever found Ben's style so infectious Maybe he helped out when the psychos were busy. He'd got the room right though — stacks of tinned food, ashtrays full of criminally wasted fags, the curtains drawn. He'd certainly made her room look like a hole-up.

'My heart went out of it when the doctor got rubbed out,' said Ben. Again Joseph drained of colour. He was like an egg-timer that needed upending every three minutes. He couldn't seem to speak even rube's words.

'You must have read about it, baby. Don't snow me. Your contact, old Dr Ostbahn, the old kraut who phoned you. Someone stuck a hypodermic through his neck.'

Joseph gulped. 'In the — market place.'

'Right.'

'But the one who phoned me wasn't Ostbahn. He only pretended to be — you remember — it was your idea. I never even knew his real name.' Joseph tried to look guileless. Better a rube than a stiff hipster. It hurt though.

'Yeah but did he know your real name? That's the big question professor. That's what you want to worry about. Because if he did and if he wrote it down, the cops are going to start filing your teeth. So where were you when the doctor got outside the needle?'

'You're joking! I didn't kill him — I never even saw him. Why should I want to kill him?'

'Ostbahn was a well-known anti-semite, anti-black, anti-socialist bastard. He wrote articles in *The Lancet* about the benevolent effect of fall-out. It's only time gone before some hot cop gets the big flash on that and starts checking on firebrands like you. He's only got to look at you, man —'Ben pointed to his badges— 'you've got motives pasted all over your lapels. My old man's A-dust man.'

This was an insult to Joseph's intelligence. He'd been played for a sucker once and the memory of that stung him to make a dangerous assertion. 'What about you then — where were you cleversticks?' He was more upset about the 'cleversticks' than any possible bullet.

'I was right here with old Carol. I never saw the doctor that day at all. You were the contact baby — me, I was only a sleeping partner.' Ben obviously didn't give a damn if he believed him or not. He had the gun.

'They'll soon find out what you've been doing,' said Joseph stoutly.

'From you?'

'What do you think I am — you think I'd go to the police?' No sense in going too far.

Ben leaned forward and thrust his face up close to Joseph's. His hot breath clouded Joseph's eyeballs. 'I don't know what you are but I'll tell you this for free. I know what you're going to be.' Joseph averted his eyes from this menacing sirocco and was suddenly, horribly aware of an inert form under the blankets of Carol's bed. Involuntarily, he gave a little quavery moan. Had he killed her too?

'You're going to be so mousy quiet that they think you're dead. You dig? Because if you finger me professor, the shit is going to hit the fan and everybody is going to catch a faceful. A contact man like you — if that's the most they can lay on you — will get five years.'

'He did know my christian name,' said Joseph, not knowing which bit to worry about first.

'Looks black, uh?' said Ben in mock sympathy. 'Well, you keep your trap shut and everything will be jake. After all, I know

I didn't do it and you tell me you didn't do it so that makes it someone else, right? Once they catch him, they'll stop looking.'

It was no good. Even if it was his last bulletin Joseph had to know. Wincing at the word 'bulletin' he nevertheless tottered over to the bed and drew the sheets back from her face. Her hair was all over her face, and in the gloom it was impossible to tell whether she was dead or alive. Hardly daring to breathe he grasped her shoulder — warm! two candles — and shook her awake. But she was different. She was alive but she could sure keep a secret. She hardly looked like Carol at all. She stank of bed and stale sweat and she was a mess.

'What — what's the matter with her?' automatically turning from her to ask Ben, but Ben only pushed him aside and sat beside her. 'Where was I last Saturday, honey?'

His hand regularly smoothed back her hair.

One of the straps of her slip had broken and the filigreed top hung down exposing one breast. Joseph couldn't take his eyes off the breast. His stare had the quality of drinking; he stood transfixed while a cocktail of fear and lust and pity ran thickly up the straw.

'You were with me.' Carol's voice had the strange resonance of the deaf.

'All day,' said Ben.

'All day.'

'So that leaves just you, professor,' said Ben smiling at Joseph and then turning his attention back to Carol. 'Carol and I are going out together. She's my girlfriend — right, baby? She got fed up with John because he couldn't do it. She says he's a cripple — got a cripple's appetites too. She gave him back his frat pin because she wouldn't give house room to no pervert's pin. Just as well she found out in time — they were practically engaged you know.' Looking up suddenly Ben intercepted Joseph's communication with the breast. 'Tell him about the foul practices in the hut.'

'I don't want to hear!'

Carol covered her eyes with her bare arm as if dazzled by light. Joseph saw that her fingernails were torn and bleedy looking. Ben placed his hand on her naked breast, his eyes fixed on Joseph as he began stroking the soft flesh. His fingers caught at the nipple and he smiled. The nipple, pinched and drawn into stiffness, stood out between his fingers, a hard purple point that seemed to be staring straight at Joseph. He knew he had to get out of here, out of this insane set-up yet he didn't move. For the first time since Joseph had woken her, she lifted her eyes, not seeing him, passing over him and up to the bare white ceiling. She began to move, arching her body up towards the imprisoned flesh and panting.

'Tell him about John, baby. Tell him about that very traumatic beach hut — he wants to know. You'll never get well unless you talk about it.'

Ben wasn't laughing now. His face was a livid white. He seemed to have forgotten that Joseph was there. He tore back the blankets from her squirming body. Joseph thought he was going to be sick. He pushed blindly for the door. On the last flight of stairs he tripped and fell heavily into the hall, his outstretched hand toppling a bicycle onto his back. He grappled with it, sobbing aloud, his hat jammed over his eyes. Ludicrously, his thumb caught on the bell and sent a small metallic ping vibrating through the house.

When he got home he locked his door and tilted a chair against it. His hands were jumping so much that he had to sit on them. Familiar record covers stared down at this crumpled little hipster. He had lost all his cool.

Forgetting everybody else's problems, how could he prove where he was on Saturday? Nobody could have seen him because he'd been in bed with a cold. He searched his mind for corroborators, square, tory or rube. Sane was all.

Then he remembered the girl next door. She would have heard the gramophone, feed a cold, not evidence but something towards establishing his whereabouts. And then his face fell. She knew about the phone calls, had even called him to answer Ostbahn that time. Perhaps she'd forgotten. More candles.

He removed the flimsy barrier against fate and stepped out into the hall. She came to the door in a candlewick dressing gown and fluffy yellow slippers like chicks. Her head came at him like a knuckle-duster, encrusted with tin curlers.

'What do you want, bumsquirt?'

Incredibly his manner became indolent, voice dripping innuendo. He couldn't afford to make a balls of this. Inside, he was a drowning man.

'Just felt like seeing you.' He offered her a cigarette.

She leaned, curlers coquettishly clanking, towards his light and shot him an up and under look that set his sphincter racing.

'You're shitting yourself about those phone calls aren't you?'

He almost fell.

'The coppers were here this morning while you were out, checking the phone number. You don't have to worry though. That's all they've got — no names. They're looking for a woman patient, see. He was an abortionist — as you know.'

He couldn't speak.

'Lucky I can be bought,' she said, helping him into her room and unbuckling his belt with a terrible mastery. There were lipstick stripes on the back of her hand.

6

Ben had been up and dressed and waiting for half an hour when the bell rang at 10am precisely. He shook Carol awake — 'Get up!' — and ran downstairs to the front door. A black man and a white man stood on the step.

'Mr Ben Herod?' asked the white man. He wore heavy Buddy Holly glasses that transcended his features, and his hair, now at 35 down to a drooped alice-band, stood out wildly curling.

'Come in,' said Ben, keeping well back from the open door.

Outside were morning sounds of milk bottles and jobbing whistlers. They came into the dark hallway, the black man delicately wiping his shoes as if they were nibs, on the mat. He was very short and thin, fastidiously dressed in a black button-to-the-neck raglan and a near brimless hat. Both men carried bulky holdalls.

'Before we go up,' said Ben, 'she's never posed before. She doesn't know what you do or why you're here. She'll do what I tell her, but I don't want you interfering.'

The white man looked annoyed. He thought it was all fixed up.

'How long is all this going to take then?' He looked at his watch.

'Look, dad,' Ben made buffers of his hands, 'just don't crowd the pace, that's all. Be patient. When I've set it up you can film all day. Shoot *Exodus* if you like.'

'I won't do no kike movie,' said the black man .

They went upstairs. At the door Ben asked for the money.

'After,' said the white man, and they went in.

'Hey!' said the white man excitedly, dropping the hold-all, shrugging out of his coat to reveal more wild black tendrils at the collar of his open-neck shirt. 'White walls, lots of light and a black and white lady. I got that feeling, Carlyle.' He put on his director's cap, a flipper cap with pouches for his clip-on sunglasses and, light meter in hand, advanced on Carol like a diviner. Carol sat on the edge of the rumpled bed and rhythmically scratched her shin. She did not look up when he held the light meter to her face and her eyes stared straight ahead when he gently lifted her chin on his fingers.

'Beautiful,' he said. 'The new Louise Brooks no less. Black hair, white body. Black and white.' He straightened up. 'That's the motif. Do you have any black sheets for a sandwich shot?'

Ben took her hand away from her shin and held it. 'You'll make yourself sore, baby.'

They all stared at the silent girl in the grimy slip but nobody asked the obvious question. The star leaned in dapper pose against the wall, legs crossed and hat tilted down over his eyes.

'There'll be no black and white motif if she ain't bathed. I'm telling you. I'm particular.'

'You'd make yourself more money if you got another star,' said Ben to the director, his face tight with hate, averted from the negro, and already speaking through a second.

'You should see my profile, white boy.' Carlyle made an airy and unseen wave of the hand that set his rings glittering.

'Leave it alone,' leaving who and what unspecified, the director had to get the show on the road. 'Stand her up,' he told Ben and then seized a handful of slip at the back to outline her body. 'She's tall but she's worth it. You'll have to use the crate, Carlyle.'

Carlyle peeled down to a sharp silk suit and a shaven head and signed off by shooting his cuffs. 'I don't wanna work with her. She's dirty and she's daft. Why can't we use a model?'

'Look, Carlyle. I'm the director so I cast this movie. I need a girl like this. She looks right. She's an original. Look at that face —' he gripped her jaw and swung her head to the critic — 'vulnerable! Sensitive! I don't need to use the leg irons or the nun's outfit because they can see she's helpless. I can get millions of flyblown models with talented yodelling snatches, so who's involved in their fight for virtue? I'll tell you — no-one. And if they're not involved we don't make money.'

'Okay, okay,' said Carlyle and went into the kitchen.

'Get her washed,' said the director. 'Comb her hair.' Wire hangers rattled down the rail as he shoved through her dresses in the curtained alcove. He tried two of them, thrusting them up against her throat for comparison with an impersonal movement like a painter's thumb and choosing at last a black and white check gingham smock with yokel x's under the bust. He dropped the reject and checked the smock for easy access through the zipped back, then he gave it to Ben. 'Black shoes,' he said — 'low heels and sling backs.' Increasingly his movements went with his hat, eyes slitting to gauge, hands chopping the air into frames, all movements abrupt as jump cuts. Now he jabbed a shop-wrapped parcel at Ben and flicked the twisted pink bow. 'Don't forget the rendables.' He stood back to admire his work — Ben, one arm holding Carol on her feet, the other laden for the purification, a livid Xmas tree for some season of hatred. 'Good,' said the director. 'Stay out of here for twenty minutes because I want to get the feel of the place. And don't come barging in. Knock.' He tried to take the edge off this with a boyish bevelled grin and then waved his eyebrows rapidly like a ventriloquist's doll, but he could see that his TAM rating stayed where it was.

'Plenty of soap !' shouted the star from the kitchen, making cutlery sounds, but Ben had gone. As he heard the door close he added — 'That man wants gutting.'

'Yes, yes, we know.' The director was getting the feel of it, the act of creation for the film of the same name. He sat on the bed, sat in the rocking chair, sat on the sofa, checked each location for light. 'Now what I want,' he spoke excitedly, 'is footage of this room. I can really,' he paced the floor, 'get something going here.'

'What a waste.' Carlyle emerged from the kitchen eating poached egg on toast. His little finger presided politely crooked over this activity.

The director had now unpacked his camera. 'Look Carlyle. I'm the director. You're the star. Let's keep it like that. I want thirty seconds of this room at the start of my movie, right? That establishes the context, then I build from there. I don't want to open with you stropping your pud, see? I'm not making movies for the jerk-off market. I make high class coffee-table eroticism and that's where the money is.'

Camera in hand, he stood on the bed, crepe shoes nearly buried in pouting eiderdown, and moved it in a practice swathe from window to wall. Then he began to shoot film, and the glass eye whirred slowly and smoothly, housed on its pelvic hinge: smooth round apples rolled onto the spool and inflated slowly into close-up in his head. 'Carlyle!' he shouted suddenly, bouncing on the mattress. 'I've got an idea. Come here! Take a bite out of this apple.'

'Man I'm eating egg.'

'Come on come on come on,' he levered at the munching negro with his lens.

'I don't like apples.'

'You can spit it out. I only want the bite out of it.'

Carlyle shifted the plate to his left hand, anchored the toast with a thumb and took a bite of apple. 'I dunno why you couldn't of bit it yourself,' he complained and spat it onto his palm and threw the chunk in the fireplace.

'Because it would have felt wrong, that's why. Because I'm the director see. I get the erotic ideas and you act them out. It would be like masturbation for me to do it.' He placed the apple back in the bowl and arranged it so that the bite touched the apple next to it and both were in a pool of light. 'Mammarian emblems,' he breathed. 'I'll tell you Carlyle, I'm going to use these as a motif. Just the shape, round, luscious, quiescent see — a woman alone. I show the apples see then I zoom in fast and reveal the bite. The Marks of the Predator. It will sort of presage your arrival. And there's the Fall and so on if they want to see that in it.'

'I done this too runny,' said the star, eating.

The director flipped his peak up to prevent shadow and zoomed in on the bite, brightening as he saw the bonus of froth anointed on the peel. 'A film starring apples,' the actor sneered a yokey sneer. 'I'd better go and oil the muscle.'

'You wait. Eat your egg.' Having drained the apples, the camera moved among the net curtains in pursuit of an entoiled and iridescent bluebottle. The director bobbed and weaved, hoovering for eroticism, regretting the fretful buzz. 'Listen to him. Buzz buzz buzz and me without sound. Taps, raindrops, clocks, pigeons' wings, boots — all crashing away in their suggestive way and I can't do a thing about it.'

He sighed and switched off the camera.

'You want me to oil up?'

'Okay. Oil the prop. And get into the overalls. You're the gas-man.

Mutiny placed pink palms on narrow hips and drew Carlyle up to his full proud-backed five foot two. 'Oh come on, man. Have a heart. I played the gasman in the last three movies. I'm not going to be typecast like this.'

'You were a window-cleaner last time.'

'It's the same thing — the same drag. Bloody boiler-suit. Can't I be a salesman, man?'

'Look, Carlyle. Listen. I've told you, this is for the English market. There's no outrage in the white collar bracket. Even vicars are dead. If we make you manual we've got all the fringe benefits of the class theme. Mucky, brutal gas-man rapes pale fragile girl — that's outrageous.'

'Why don't you use a ape?' Carlyle unpacked the boiler-suit and glared at it. It looked lacklustre despite his alterations, the padded shoulders, the button-down collar, tapered ruler pocket.

'I haven't got an ape,' replied the director and regretted it at once. Carlyle let the implications lie fallow however, not choosing to quarrel with his bread and butter. He took the boiler-suit and his make-up case, moroccan leather, the name in gold, and retired to the kitchen. In this green room's unsuitable clutter the black luminary dusted off a humble stool and sat down to transform his profile.

There was a large mirror over the sink and he unhooked it from its nail and placed it on the breadboard, propped against a loaf. From his make-up case he took a chamois leather cloth and, with almost reverent care, he huffed and buffed the impurities away. On the breadboard he laid his clean white initialled hand-towel, and on that he arranged tubes and jars of his cosmetics. He sat and waited for the elevation with that blind faith of man in the mechanistic.

Soon the spirit descended upon him. He arose and dropped his trousers. It was awe inspiring, man and member in arbitrary combination like the centaur. Even he could not bring himself to look upon the sight, but with averted eyes he beheld in the mirror the gothic majesty of Real Presence.

He began to limber up. Pilgrim-shuffling in his anklet trousers, he presented himself to the mirror in a cinemascopic range of portrayals. To unheard Debussy he gently drifted his image across the glass in a series of limpid passes; every movement was perfect. Off screen his mood brightened and, turning, his legs began to pizzicato in their silken confines. He spun past the mirror like a cossack and finished the revel by springing the chuckling member up onto the screen in a limbless star-jump. Then irised out, very pleased, plopped bare buttocks onto the cold wood of the stool, and began his usual inspection.

'I gotta spot!'

The director spun about to see the star on the profane side of the kitchen doorway. His shirt was caught up and held under his chin and his trousers were cloth pools. He was quite beside himself.

Whenever the director entered the Presence he experienced cringing humility. His fingers itched up to the brim of his flippercap; only his annoyance with himself over this prevented scenes of abasement. Now he bent and looked.

'What do you think it is?' A very worried star.

'Nothing. Let's see. Just a spot.'

'*Just* a spot, the man says! It's symptomatic!'

'Of?'

'Of this whole crummy set-up is of what. Of you hiring that grubby ofay chick, that loony, to be in my movie. Of me having to unrobe in that loony's grubby kitchen. Of you wasting money and time — my time — snapping flies and apples in that loony's room. I'm very sensitive, you know that. I'm an artist. That's why I've got this psychosomatic spot.'

The director sighed. 'You're very unfair,' he said. 'Everybody is off-colour sometimes. It's not my fault.'

'I regard off-colour as very cheap.' He turned huffy buttocks on his colleague and shuffled away.

The director's face, arranged on mollifying lines, came round the kitchen door.

'You can use the light meter,' he said, thinking the burgers of Calais. The black neck did not move, brain brooding on blemish. He put the meter down on the initialled towel and had started to withdraw when the star sullenly spoke.

'You keep me in long shot, you hear.'

'Yes, Carlyle.' Thinking, *like hell*, also *kiss my arse*. He sat on the table and began thinking out the structure of his film in terms of chalk marks and angles. He wished his star was taller so that he needn't lie down to get menace footage.

Carlyle picked up the light meter and checked it against his Presence. The light meter made him feel like a realer star than the real star he knew he was. He wished he could read it. Figuring, he decided that a light make-up on the Presence would be a good idea, turning his natural body-colour to emphatic mascara. He uncapped the No. 9 and uncowled the Presence, but before they met, thoughts of the spot returned, and the spirit left him.

'This spot,' he said, his voice so crushed that the director hardly heard him.

'I said,' he said, 'this spot.'

'Make-up,' shouted the director, engrossed.

'Huh.' Carlyle doodled aimlessly. 'I can't raise one.'

Panic seized the director's voice. 'What's that?'

'I said, I can't raise one. I'm not in the mood.'

'Carlyle. You're a professional. Try again now for God's sake.'

Very depressed star: 'It's no good.'

'Concentrate!'

'I am doing.'

'Maybe it's too close in there. Is it too close in there? You want a window open? His shoes are too tight. Carlyle — are you wearing those tight shoes again?'

'It's none of that. All that's okay. I'm just depressed.'

'Oh God.'

'Do you ever get to thinking maybe there's no point in this? What's it all for? After all.'

The alarmed director looked down on the bowed black neck. 'Most people think that every so often, Carlyle, but it's different for you. I can't see how you can ever, ever doubt. Because it's not just you anymore. You have your public. Now me — I get depressed sometimes but that doesn't matter. I'm replaceable. I know that. Without you I'd be just one more lousy commercial cameraman. Clapper-boy even. You can't ever let yourself get depressed because of your public. They pay to see you, Carlyle, and you know why? Star quality. Every guy in the audience is up there with you, letting them have it, doing the old thing with Carlyle. And the women! Carlyle, I'll tell you. I've sat in the audience and I've watched them in your movies. They can't sit still — they really eat up your profile, I kid you not. Have you ever seen an audience watching anyone else's movies? You owe it to yourself to do that. It's a farce. It's an uproar. "Gertcha, we can see the buckles!" "He musta dozed off." Stuff like that — the big horse laugh. But your movies! Reverent. That's the word. You dominate. You know what I got yesterday? Slipped my mind, a letter from the Civil Rights people. They've sent a cheque to keep you off the screen.

'How's that,' cried the star turning round, proudly smiling.

'About time,' said the spent director, a crystal row of sweat-beads along his cap-brim, his fingers itching up to touch the place.

In the bathroom Ben stood staring in revulsion at the bloodied palms of his hands. This time it had come over him without warning. He felt sick, strained in the guts.

Carol's head lay on the rim of the bath and her body seemed to melt in pink wavy lines through the steaming water. When he spoke to her she opened her eyes but she didn't look at him. She looked like a five-year-old: hair in a topknot, face flushed and sullen, she would ride through the adult night in a piggyback bound for a sheet-saving pee. As he watched, her eyes began to melt big fat silent tears.

'Shut up,' he said and bent over the bath to wash the blood from his hands. Underwater, his hand felt for her thighs and gently squeezed. She just went on crying with that some mindless five-year-old incontinence.

'Look,' said Ben, holding up the shop-wrapped parcel. 'Pretties. A present for you.'

It was packed in gold paper, sellotaped along the edge with a superfluous twist of pink ribbon around it. Carol made no move to take it but she oozed a few more tears. Ben gave up and sat on the bathroom chair. Being in the bathroom made it the bathroom chair. Nothing in the bathroom was special except the bath. The mirror had come to the rooming house from a foreclosed barber-shop and advertised a brand of hair grease; the rubber bathmat was palette-shaped to fit a lavatory. Some genius had papered the walls and the steam had, as steam will, demoralised the fit so that it hung in loose floral bulges like a portrait of O Wilde by D Gray. Sodden pieces of wallpaper always clogged the plughole. Hot water cost a shilling.

'Today is the last day baby,' said Ben. 'And then I'm going away. I might even miss you, you never know. Boy, the kicks we've had together. I nearly dislocated my jaw yawning. Now if I had a photo I'd give it to you so's you'd remember me right. You know how I am, all mush inside.' He gingerly felt the little half-moon cuts on his palm. They were stinging from the water. 'No, on second thoughts I think we'll skip the photo bit. Not a good idea at all. I have to be so careful about my fool heart ruling my head, especially now with the fuzz breaking out their drop-handlebars and all.' He smiled and leaned across to unstrap the watch from her limp wrist.

'You still don't know what time it is do you baby. You stay that way. Stupid.' He kissed her softly on the forehead.

'When I'm gone you'll forget all about me. After all, you've got some of your own things going now. There's the addiction for one thing, and photography. You'll wake up and find the two mice and the pumpkin outside your door again. It'll all seem like a dream.' Ben was gazing off into the distance like a medium. He seemed to be talking to himself and his American accent had disappeared.

'I'll fix you up with John again baby. I can get him back.'Good old John, eh. You can sew leather patches on his elbows for him. 'Get a new elastic band for your pony-tail. Get married. It'll be hard on your finger baby but he is steady. You'll be very liberal — go round telling people that hanging is wrong. Yeah, you keep that bit up honey. That's noble work.'

Beyond knowing, Carol floating achieved immortal longings. In the porcelain womb of the bath she had reversed creation to become, unforming, her limits dissolving, lymph. Not happy lymph, not wistful lymph but just plain old lymph lymph. A lymph nymph. Carol wasn't Ben any more. Carol was bathwater. Out and into, went her body, and regret and anticipation sank without a trace in the busy mixture. There were needle marks in her upper arm.

'I can make all this disappear for you, baby. I can rub it all out. I can do it too. It's my job. The Great Eraser.'

Ben held up his hand as if in benediction and closed his eyes. 'You never sat on the platform that night so we never met. You got on the last train and went home and wrote that the sea had been grey and the sky full of candy floss. You never walked in the fields at night because nobody you knew had a car. You slept all night and stayed up all day like people do.'

Carol was conscious only of the drone of his voice. There was no place for him in the new order of things. Then he seized her hands and pulled her upright onto her feet Her dreaming flesh streamed back through his fingers, outraged, cords and strings of water breaking from her, but he held her fast. He towelled her roughly and her head wobbled on its limp stalk. Fluid welled up in her eyes and rolled down her cheeks. Her arms hurt her, hurt someone, she didn't know; hurt. Now suddenly she could see him, grotesquely jolted against wedges of paper flowers, he was a flat white cut-out in a kaleidoscope. His mouth flew open, shook open into red and she heard, understanding nothing, the raw inhuman sound of his screaming.

'He did it! I'll kill him I'll —' His arm was a shuddering crescent above her head. 'Touched you! Touched you with his shit-filth hands and you let him!' He thrust the harsh scrubbing brush into her hands and crushed her fingers around it.

'Scrub! Scrub it off! Quick — use the brush! Do it all over all — *everywhere*! Harder. *Harder than that — bleed! bleed it out!* He touched you there. Filth! Black shit filth I'll kill him, *I'll kill him!*'

7

The jangling of the bell through the empty house brought John from his sleep, sliding down the shiny pole into the reality of his rumpled bed. He groped for the alarm and then remembered that he had not wound it for a week. That made it the front door bell. He half-fell out of bed onto the cold lino, and pressing his face to the window, looked down on the empty porch.

A six o'clock sun shone on the dry concrete, freezing the dull pools in the gutter to mercury, the rinsed milk bottles to clubs of ice. Diamonds of grit sparkled seductively on the pavement below, but John was not tempted. Only a fool would venture abroad in this mineral world, at this un-human hour. There was no sign of his caller. He hopped back into bed.

But he couldn't get back to sleep. He lay there thinking about things as they occurred to him, following nothing, unselective. He felt very strange. Sick almost. His father, Carol, Joseph passed through his mind like figures in a striking clock. He watched them without emotion. His head felt as if it were stolen goods, hot, snatched and urgent on the pillow. Now he recalled a nursery tale from his childhood. A thief steals some merchandise — a ring perhaps or a goose — and as he runs through the windy town the thing (the goose?) screams for help from between the guilty hands. There was a picture in the book which had terrified him. The thief was blue and red; his hands were red. There were no citizens in the windy town. A cat crouched on a brimming dustbin wolfing at lumps of rag. The lid had fallen off, was still falling, to the cobbles. Thief! Thief! Master!

It was no better in the bathroom. Surfaces, chrome, plastic, porcelain rang against his eyes. He was nauseously aware of being flesh amid mineral, all rosy and vulnerable for their sharp edges. He moved with exaggerated care. The tumbler perhaps to tumble — in its nature — burst in the bath, wound the cringing foot, wound opening under water, a dream of nausea. Call me a semantic fool. He washed and dried selected orifices with baby-care, shivering in the pearly light.

He opened the door of his father's room and released an eddy of stale, closeted air. What he expected to find there he didn't know. Nothing had changed. On the floor lay the cold hot-water bottle where he had left it a week ago. It struck him forcefully that it would remain there, beached bladder, high and dry in linoleum latitudes, two feet from the bed and three from the wall for ever, unless he chose to move it. Everything in the house would stay where he left it now, for no good reason, forgotten reason, a little Pompeii in the suburbs. He felt like having the room sealed up. The double bed shone faintly with sunlight along its iron shank, unflocked skeleton, its unlapped sleepers reunited at last in a bony embrace.

The view from this window was over the backyards. A neighbour crunched over the cinders in overalls, yawning immensely, blind to the familiar route to work. A handful of sparrows, dusty as old carpet, fled before his unhinged jaws. Plump sachets of yolk had popped in that mouth behind the discreet screen of the *Daily Mirror*. John let the curtain fall back into place and left the room.

On the hall mat his eyes fell on a plain unaddressed envelope. He slit it with his thumbnail and took out six photos. There was no other message.

Now the six photos were spread before him on the kitchen table. He thought he was going mad. They were his dreams. They had come to life, hideously alive and independent of him, jerking out the convulsions that he had willed for her in the hot dark of his bed. It was as if his jerking hand had pierced her limbs with wires. He covered his eyes with a shaking hand and it seemed for a moment as if he were going to faint. He was the thief. He had been caught in the bright white magic flashlight of day with a snowy goose clutched in his fingers, and his face was fixed in a ghastly corded glaring grimace. He could see her face looking up at him — Carol staring mindlessly at him and not seeing, held there at the neck by thin black fingers.

He was guilty. He felt it everywhere; in the pressure of the chair along his thighs, in the ache of his elbows on the table. His eyes opened on objects. He alone was guilty; he alone was flesh and that flesh had willed degradation on another. He burned with shame and in the general movement of blood along his veins a specific tumescence occurred which confirmed to him his diseased sexuality. He wanted to turn all the keys, close the curtains and nail them in place, bury his head under pillows and die, throttling on his guilt like a dog in his vomit.

Someone knew him more intimately than he had believed possible. Someone who had pointed his lens directly into the most secret chambers of his mind. He had delivered the photos to him like meat thrown to a leper. No message was necessary. The caller had run. John tried to think rationally. She had told this person about him, about the beach, and he had known exactly how to use it to hurt him. What was he after? He had calculated his reaction to the last spasm of shame but to what purpose, for what motive? Was he, John, meant to do something more? Come gunning, stamp lens and photographer to pulp under righteous heels; slash his own wrists?

John seized the photos and ran upstairs. He no longer knew if he was acting from pity or from vengeance or from a burning need for confrontation. He was acting. Even allowing for the double meaning that was miraculous. He was going to Carol. But he was not sure whether he had chosen or whether, unimaginably, he had been programmed by his tormentor as he had programmed her.

Fifty miles out of the city Ben pulled the big car off the road onto a carpet of leaves. He sat holding the wheel and staring at the traffic slamming past. A continuous flash of metal hurtled past his elbow a few feet away. Bright lines pulled out of speed on the peripheries of his vision. Objects became their function; cars abstracted into movement, became a horizontal morse on the road. It seemed very beautiful to him.

Six-forty-five. On the seat beside him lay the briefcase, lid unbuckled, the opening towards him where the gun was. He turned on the radio and listened to the weather forecast. 'Snow,' said Ben smiling.

After a while he decided. At six-fifty the one car that really stuck out in a crowd was heading back to the city.

She was sitting in the rocking chair. She didn't look up when he closed the door. She didn't know that he had run out on her or why he had come back. She saw only the briefcase. That was all that existed.

Gently, Ben took the scissors from her cold bluish fingers. He examined the punctures she had made in her arms. Most of them were slight but a couple went deeper and were torn probably as the points jerked out. Carol started crying like a grizzly kid, on and on, flatly, without vehemence. She was still wearing the thick film make-up, a sad/funny clown's face, now blotched and red under the white. Streaks of black ran down her cheeks.

'Yoohoo honey. It's me — back from the office. Did you have a good day?' He bit his thumb, studying her.

'You don't seem to have much on the ball today. You're not yourself. You've been very distant with me since last Thursday. Wednesday, I tell a lie. It's getting me down. What's up? Huffy? Consty? Preggie? Junkie?' Ben paused between each question and cocked his head as if stepping back between brush-strokes.

'You could be civil. Just because you're a pregnant junkie. We've all got troubles. Self-centred is what.'

He turned away and went into the kitchen, still talking quietly against the unbroken sound of Carol's crying. He ran hot water into a basin and tore a handful of cotton wool from the roll. There was a tin of elastoplast in the cutlery drawer.

I bet you wonder why I came back.' He started for the door laden with articles and saw her on her knees frantically pawing through the contents of his briefcase. His instruments fell in a heap, bottles, needles and coil strewn all over the floor. The briefcase had been dumped upside down.

He grabbed her hair and pulled her off balance away from the syringe before her out-thrust hands could connect. As she toppled weakly onto her side, he bent to retrieve it. Out of the corner of his eye he saw the big gun in her two hands.

The coldness of the brass doorknob stuck to his sweating palm like a burn. John could not seem to find the will to turn it and enter the room, the lists, the trying place appointed. It was very dark and damp-smelling on the landing and the sound of his own breathing reminded him farcically of Tone in the well.

Then he heard the explosion. Felt, rather, the huge impact of the brass on his flesh as the first bullet struck the door. He flung himself back against the wall and saw the door suddenly splinter, bristling up white daggers of wood from its varnished surface. The noise— he couldn't tell if it was one single reverberating explosion or a chain of clangour— ran through his jerking body like voltage. Even when it was over he could not recall where he was or what he had come to do. For a moment it seemed to him that he was in some forge, foundry, cavern of the Industrial Revolution, was flickering small and barefoot through steam and hurtling pistons.

The door would not come open and he had to lean his full weight against the panel before he felt the obstacle slowly give way. Ben had fallen at the door and, dying, slid a bloody swathe across the lino before the opening door.

John knelt beside him and saw dumbly the great ragged exit-holes in Ben's chest before he raised his head and saw her. Carol sitting as if before a movie. A revolver loosely held in her hands. He spoke to her, saying her name in a voice that sounded too weak to reach her now. She looked at him without any expression, her eyes flat and blackly animal under her ragged cowl of hair. Everywhere that pearly unreal light turned the room white as a spun spectrum of colours is white.

It was difficult to take the gun from her for the fingers of both hands were laced around the trigger, and he had to apply strong pressure to each hand in turn. There were two live bullets left in the chamber; he was tucking the gun into his belt before he realised. Not the broken syringe on the floor; not the stab wounds on her soft, blue-bruised arms; not even his tormentor dead. The gun was a Colt .45. John stared at it. It was beautiful, the most beautiful thing he had ever seen, an object of glory. The myth of courage and virility lay cold and true in his hand, weighed his hand down with power. This was what he had come for. He had found his rôle.

He took out the photos of Carol and let them flutter down onto the corpse. Ben stared up sightlessly, his face a mask of agony and horror, Ben who had used everybody, buried beneath a mask, all used up. John realised that it was all settled now; better, settled in a convention cleaner and truer than life. He had shot him down like a dog for the prostitution of his lover.

He knew instinctively that feet would come running now, voices shouting, sucked by natural force into the vacuum left by the explosion. People would flood back and destroy the pattern. Oh yes. He knew himself, his weakness. He would help to spoil it, revoke, rescind, recant. But he mustn't! He gripped the gun, his gun, tightly in his fist.

He had one more thing to do here. He trailed the backs of his fingers absently down Carol's cheek, not feeling its smooth warmth, feeling no pity, no love. Observance of gesture was enough for him now, enough for this. 'Temple Drake,' he said and smiled. Squatting in front of her chair, he sighted on her eyes and released a short hard punch to her jaw, lifting her and the chair over backwards, unblocking with a flash — *POW! BLAM!* — the dazzling new sun. She lay on the rug with her dirty slip wrinkled up over tight belly like a partly sloughed skin. Her attitude had the random, flung obscenity of a police photograph and it struck him that he had posed her again.

Checking her pulse, he heard them.

Voices raised in the hall. Feet on the stairs. No time for guilt now. He came through the doorway like a bull, bellowing. He had a blurred impression of red holes opening at him and then receding in confusion at the sight of his gun slashing through air at them, then he was past, hammering down the stairs head over heels almost and into the street.

People were running towards him as in a dream, completely absorbed in that action, were the action in inseparable plurality. And he was running. He threw up his arm and took aim and the mass parted. Some dropped to the ground, others dived into doorways. But he couldn't shoot into them, that famous freest act, instead, swinging the barrel round to a parked car bearing jokey transfer bullet-holes, he fired two jokey bullets into the windscreen.

Running now down the street, lungs bursting, laughing like a madman. Beside him ran the great ones. Bogart running, gun in hand to his death-falling witness. Belmondo down that final boulevard, dying, a fag burning in his mouth. Cybulski sniffing his own blood among the washing and running to his death on the crap heap. And Billy going for an empty holster. They ran with John. He held on hard to them, to his movie ending.

He swerved out, tiring now, onto the flyover and ran up the gradient treading cats-eyes. Ahead jigged Technicolour notices.

Slow Down. No Learners. Behind him horns began to sound and he staggered to the left of the road. The great ones wouldn't come! Red flames leaped behind his eyes. 'Yes go on burn it all!' he shouted as the urchins pronged furniture and tree-boughs and petrol onto the bonfire. 'Burn it all up!' They circled and whooped behind protective dustbin lids. The flames shimmered up, leaping higher, hotter, creating a vacuum that sucked at property, that tore possessions from their places with the suction plop of departing eyeballs. His father's knuckles whitened around sideboard handles and from his screaming mouth ran hanging gobs of plastic, pink cysts containing teeth, a biteful of tiles from the roof…

Ten ton of steel hit him as he reached the top of the ramp. It broke upon him like a gigantic wave and it broke him. His eyes did not see the spire of the church below, the double spire, nor the kite trapped in the branches that were clearly visible from the top of the flyover.

The lorry driver flung on his air-brakes and the huge eight-wheel lorry jarred to a halt. The driver, a Korean War veteran in greasy overalls and an open-neck check shirt knelt down beside the body and vomited. The radiator had impressed the pattern of its metal grill on John's face, breaking his skull and stopping his heart. A motor-cycle cop pulled off his gauntlet and inserted a hand under the bloody combat jacket, just a formality, and then held back the traffic on the ramp until the body could be cleared.

Drivers craned through their windscreens for a look and then sat back ashen faced, staring bleakly down at their dashboards. Further back, not knowing the cause of the hold up, drivers beat their gloved hands impatiently on their steering wheels, lit up angry cigarettes. The fringes of the expanding blockage parted to let the ambulance through.

That Easter there were 23 road deaths in the county. John was number 19. In the morgue Mr Reed failed at first to recognise him. He had a hell of a job cutting through the finger tendons to free the empty gun for the police laboratory.

8

'Well, I blame him. It's all very well to say that he was highly strung, but it seems to me that he was the author of all your misfortunes. Your mother and I read some of his letters in your drawer when you were in hospital. Now don't look at me like that — we felt we ought to know everything. You're our only child after all.'

They sat on the park bench, fingers loosely entwined, a middle-aged man in a business suit and a very pregnant young woman. 'I don't think that was very nice.' But she didn't seem annoyed, just quietly sat there smiling at the children playing on the grass.

'I think we're out of the realms of nice, Carol.'

'Are we?' she said. She didn't know. She had a great sense of well-being, of everything in its ordered place. It was ludicrous to worry about whose baby she was carry.ing, John's, Ben's, or perhaps the black man's — it was part of her now, the centre where she most perfectly *was*. Everything else was trivial.

'He had a diseased imagination. Filthy. Sick. I wonder that you didn't see that. If you hadn't got mixed up with him, you would never have — done what you did with the Other.'

Carol wondered vaguely what she had done with the Other. Of course she'd read the newspaper accounts of the sordid business but none of it seemed to apply to her. They had fitted it all together like a — why not? — she'd finished with writing — like a jigsaw. Ben killed Ostbahn. John killed Ben and was killed in the road. Ben was an abortionist. He had taken dirty photos of her; that was why John killed him.

The weight of the sun on her closed eyelids stirred something, a faint orange fluttering beyond memory. It lasted only a moment, as brief as the blank after-image of the children and the geraniums that she had carried on her retina when her eyelids closed. That sensation was all that was left of Ben, sensation merchant, and it too was subsumed in the slow smiling warmth of her happiness. It was all erased as he had promised.

Her father studied her uptilted face and worried again about her sanity. One didn't smile like that after a nightmare. He cleared his throat.

'What bothers me is why that one came back after he'd got away. The police say that he'd been seen in that flashy car fifty miles away that very morning.'

He was asking her really, and his motives were unclear even to himself. Perhaps to jolt her out of this vacancy onto normal paths of expiation and catharsis; very much a preoccupation of his generation. He was a good father and had shut the door on the reporters, set his back against the neighbours, only to find, painfully, that she didn't need him and didn't notice. Carol said: 'The papers said that John was in love with me.'

'No no. I'm talking about the other one.'

'Ben? The papers said that he was mad. He might have returned to abort me or because he loved me too, they weren't sure. Or perhaps even to see what John was going to do about the photos.'

'What do you think?' He looked very directly at her, trying to elicit a personal response.

'I don't know,' she said with a puzzled frown, puzzled at his asking her. 'Let me straighten this for you.' She extended her hand towards the knot of his tie, but was side-tracked by a tiny ladybird badge in his lapel. The tie stayed crooked.

'Why do you wear this?'

'It's for charity. You've seen it before.' So had the speaker, yet he nevertheless creased up his neck to squint down at it. His face looked very old and dried up and lined in the bright sunlight. That aspect always made her love him.

'Bearing witness, sort of thing?' she asked him slyly, and he remembered the family quarrels when she accused him of being all appearances and he told her that she was a beatnik. That all seemed a long time ago.

'It impresses the Joneses,' he laughed.

They sat together very comfortably and watched the children playing. Red buses could be seen over the tops of the bushes. A yob in a polka dot shirt and clip-on braces was playing his transistor. Carol thought that if she had a boy she would call him Heathcliff.